KU-383-771

CATHERINE DARBY

ZABILLET
OF THE SNOW

WARWICKSHIRE
COUNTY LIBRARY

CONTROL No.

Complete and Unabridged

LINFORD
Leicester

First published in Great Britain in 1990 by
Robert Hale Limited
London

First Linford Edition
published 1999
by arrangement with
Robert Hale Limited
London

The right of Catherine Darby to be identified
as the author of this work has been asserted
by her in accordance with the
Copyright, Designs and Patents Act, 1988

Copyright © 1990 by Catherine Darby
All rights reserved

British Library CIP Data

Darby, Catherine, *1935 –*
    Zabillet of the snow.—Large print ed.—
    Linford romance library
    1. Love stories
    2. Large type books
    I. Title
    823.9′14 [F]

    ISBN 0–7089–5468–5

Published by
F. A. Thorpe (Publishing) Ltd.
Anstey, Leicestershire
Set by Words & Graphics Ltd.
Anstey, Leicestershire
Printed and bound in Great Britain by
T. J. International Ltd., Padstow, Cornwall

This book is printed on acid-free paper

1

Write down everything that I tell you to write, good Sister, and afterwards make two fair copies of the words. When I am dead one shall be buried with me and the other placed in whatever nook or cranny it may please the Abbess to designate. If I had ever learned the art of writing I could have spared you this task but when I was a girl it was not considered desirable for females to have overmuch learning lest it give them notions above their station in life. I could have told them that I was born with notions above my station with or without the writing. Ah, a little smile curves your mouth within the wimple. You know exactly what I mean. Yet perhaps not, for you are twenty-one? twenty-two? You have not lived half your span. And I have lived twenty years more than mine. In this year of Grace Thirteen Hundred and Ninety-Three I have attained my grand climacteric. Sixty-three. Seven times nine making a six and a three, both magical numbers and the two adding again to nine. Yes, you do well to look impressed. Sixty-three is a great age. And I have a fancy to live some months longer, to tell my story. If I do not then who is left to record what happened? Who is left to care? Not Reynaud, not Jacques, not Benet or Alain. Certainly not Alain. I remember the first time I saw Alain, coming towards me with the sun at his back and myself standing black against the snow. They don't have winters like that any longer.

No, that is not the place to start. In the universe God decreed order and man defied Him. Let me not compound the fault by bringing more disorder. You shall have the tale plain, child. It is snowing now beyond the window and little flurries of it blow through the open space and dot your veil. So life goes around in a circle. Yes, as you say, this cold weather will keep the plague at bay. The plague is a summer visitor on the whole though the Great Plague took no account of seasons. It rampaged and romped and rotted at every season.

But that was later. I must speak of the beginning, tell you how it was. In the convent we live a lie. We blot out our pasts and say we only began to live when Our Lord's wedding ring was placed upon our hand. And that is a lie, Sister. We lived before and that wedding ring cancels nothing. All our past is held still under our carefully blank faces and lowered eyes. So with my past. And whether it be a sign of age or not I remember that past more clearly than I can recall the events of a week ago.

I was born on the first day of May in the year of Grace, Thirteen Hundred and Thirty. I was given the name Zabillet which is the local term for Isabella or Elizabeth. Local was the village of Fromage — ah, you are smiling again, but our cheeses were the finest for miles around.

I see it still without even closing my eyes. Fromage climbs up the side of a steep hill which is crowned by the stone fortress of the lords of La Neige. Lords of Snow. An ancient line that ruled those valleys and sharp crests of rock when the Merovingian kings reigned over the south. The family had dwindled somewhat, so many of the young men rushing to the Crusades and never coming home, so many girls marrying into other families. By the time I was born the La Neige had dwindled into the person of the Lady Petronella and her grandson who was ten years old.

My own parents had lived all their lives in the straggling village that climbed up to the fortress. My father was called Jean d'Aude because his own father came from that region. He was about thirty years old when I was born and well respected for our house was built of stone with shingles on the roof, and there were separate quarters for the animals. My mother was twenty years old and I was her third child, with two brothers, Reynaud and Jacques, five and two years my senior respectively. Nobody had marked the exact days of their births, but as I was born on a day sacred to Our Lady the day was remembered. Father Hubert wished me to be named Marie in Her honour but my mother had promised her mother as she lay dying that she would call her eldest daughter after her so that her memory would not fade. She had been a harsh woman and nobody particularly wanted to preserve her memory but a death-bed promise ought to be kept and there was always the danger my grandmother might come back and haunt us if she didn't get her own way.

I have heard it said that the first seven years of life trace the pattern of all that is to come. Perhaps that's so. Perhaps even when I was toddling round holding on to my mother's apron I was drawing the pattern on which I would weave the threads of my existence. The first thing I remember then is the warm smell of my mother's breasts. She was round and merry eyed and had plenty of milk. In the year I was three our sow farrowed and died and left only one piglet alive, and my mother suckled the little creature with me turn and turn about and we both thrived.

She put me in to sleep with the piglet too because my cradle was wide and lined with straw, and I remember snuggling down with it under the blanket and giggling because it rooted about in my neck with its little pink snout. I was sorry when it was killed but its meat was very good. My father said it was the milk feeding gave it such a fine flavour, and then he pinched my cheek and said:

'Margot, when this one is weaned her flesh will be even tastier, eh?'

I recall the feeling of my father's hard hand against my cheek and his eyes creased up from the smoke of the fire and the cold terror that ran through me until he laughed and my mother laughed too, but softer, saying,

'Jean, don't tease the child.'

I knew all the time he was teasing but part of me feared that he might not be. I always felt like that about my father. He was a genial man but there was something sleeping at the back of his eyes that I never wished to waken.

My mother was different. There were no dark places in her nature. She was all curves and merriment with a laugh that sounded as if little bells hung from her teeth. When she was very happy she sang and when something bad happened she wept. She had been an only child which perhaps had accounted for her mother's sourness, but that sourness had been buried with old Zabillet and my mother had brought to her marriage two hectares of land and all the contents of her mother's domus.

That domus stood a little way outside the village proper since old Zabillet — so called to distinguish her from me, her granddaughter — had never been on good terms with her neighbours. It stood still, poised between the village and the river, its shingled roof needing repair but its walls solid yet.

'When Zabillet marries she shall have it as dowry,' my mother said.

'What of the boys? Are they to be landless?' my father demanded.

'They will have the wits to find rich wives,' she said. 'If they are as handsome as you, my Jean, they will have no difficulty in finding wives.'

Little as I was I followed the drift of her reasoning. Reynaud and Jacques would have no trouble in making marriages, but I would need my grandmother's domus if anyone were to be persuaded to offer for me. I supposed it was because of my hair. Judas hair as red as the cheeks of an apple, springing thick and wiry from my head and curling to my waist. Red hair was looked upon askance in our district. The Iscariot had been red-haired and so had the Magdalene and though she had reformed her early life hadn't been too savoury.

I have mentioned Lady Petronella La Neige. She lived in the castle and never came down into the village, but sent her steward to collect the lod and ventes taxes, the quete donation levied upon every domus, the albergue which had to be paid by those who lodged in other people's houses. We knew little of her but she was frequently the topic of conversation.

'They say she washes her face in milk to preserve her complexion. She is nearly fifty and has the skin of a young girl.'

'Lady Petronella has guests up at the castle. Cousins from Avignon.'

'That will be on her mother's side. They are related to the lords of Foix, you know.'

Everybody talked about Lady Petronella but few saw her; fewer still had actually spoken to her or entered the portals of the fortress that rose against the skyline. Her house servants had come with her from her native Lorraine and kept themselves to themselves. Her son had been in the habit of riding through the village, stopping now and then to greet someone. He had had a pleasant smile and people had said that things would change when he came of age. Castle and village would grow closer together and, in hard winters, he would remit the taxes. But he had gone away into France at fifteen and died there of the coughing sickness and after a year or two his wife had followed him and Lady Petronella had travelled north and brought back her grandson.

Benet La Neige was ten years old when I was born, so though I grew up with the sound of his name in my ears he had almost certainly never heard mine.

When I was seven my mother bore another daughter, the long-awaited Marie. My father took the boys up into the hills until it was all over, and I was left to my own devices.

'Go to the church and pray,' Bernadetta ordered, pushing me out of doors. 'Now don't screw up your face at me. If the wind changes you will stay like that for the rest of your life.'

There wasn't a breath of wind, but Bernadetta had a hard hand, so I smoothed out my features and went out. To tell the truth I wasn't sorry to be sent away. My mother was crying out with the pangs of the birthing and the women crowding about her pallet were crying out in sympathy.

I went down the track and turned left on to the narrower track at the end of which our church stood. It was a wooden building with a roof of close thatch, a long rectangle with a domus at one end where Father Hubert lived. He was very old, past forty and white-haired, with a bent back and gnarled hands. He worked his own patch of land and didn't take mistresses, though in his youth it was said he had lived with a woman.

The door of his house was open and I could hear voices issuing forth. I knew the voices. The harsh strong voice belonged to Father Hubert; the thinner voice was that of Israel, the Jew.

You look shocked that we should have a Christ-killer in the village. Well, God knows I can never hope to excuse that, but Israel wasn't like other Jews. Not that we knew any. But we knew he couldn't be like the others of his race. He had come into Fromage before I was born, a stick in his hand and a knapsack on his back and rags about his feet. My mother had told me about it.

'Nobody knew what to do. We felt sorry for the poor man and gave him food and a pair of boots, but we knew that it was our duty to kill him, only that would have been a waste of the bread and cheese he'd eaten and of the boots. Gilbert said he didn't fancy taking them back from a dead man.

We were arguing about it and then someone thought to send for Father Hubert who came all in a rush with his gown tucked up and a slice of meat in his hand. He listened and then he had a few words with the Jew — he spoke Occitan very badly. Anyway Father Hubert said he could stay, that he was probably descended from those half-dozen Jews who had tried to stop the Crucifixion and wasn't like the rest of them. And Israel stayed. In the village but not really of it, since though he was lodged with the Widow Foret and worked her land for her, he often took off unexpectedly for days and weeks at a time.

'He is doomed to wander,' Father Hubert explained to us. 'All of his race are doomed to wander.'

He always wandered back sooner or later however, leaner and browner. My mother said he went up into the hills to pray. My father said he went up into the hills to pay for the services of one of Fat Berthe's girls, it being well known that Jews were supposed to indulge their carnal appetites at regular intervals. That made things difficult for him since any Christian woman having carnal relations with a Jew had her head cut off. Probably Fat Berthe's girls didn't mind the risk.

On this afternoon he and Father Hubert were deep in discussion. It was Father's earnest desire to convert him, since when every Jew is converted Jesus will come again in glory. Now he was hard at it, his rich voice throbbing.

'Can you not at least admit that God Incarnate might be born as a child into His own created world?'

'I would quarrel with your term Incarnate since that presupposes that the Creator — blessed be His Name — becomes part of the material world when the Creator is Pure Spirit.'

'Spirit becoming Flesh,' Father Hubert insisted.

I coughed and they both looked through the open door.

'Ah, Zabillet, how is your mother?'

14

Father Hubert said. 'Has her labour begun yet?'

'I was sent to pray,' I told him.

'So pray,' said Father Hubert, smiling at me. 'When you have prayed come back here and I will give you a fine red apple.'

For a fine red apple I'd have said long prayers. I bobbed my head in the polite way my mother had taught me and ran towards the church.

Our church was not a rich one with fine decorations such as some of the other villages had. That was because the La Neige family worshipped in their own chapel within the fortress and so saw no reason to give money to the village church. It was a pretty church for all that, with the inside of the walls whitewashed and painted with the great archangels. The paintings had faded over the years. Poor St Gabriel had almost vanished into the surrounding whitewash, and Father Hubert kept hinting that someone ought to touch him up a bit. Brune had tried but he had only succeeded in giving the poor archangel a bit of a squint, so one was never sure which way he was looking. The altar was of stone and there were relics of saints buried under it. At one side of the altar opposite the Perpetual Lamp was a statue of Our Lady of Fromage. You have not heard of Her under that title. Oh, the local legend was very well attested. It had happened centuries before when our village didn't even have a name. A poor shepherd had been driving his flock south and a blizzard had come upon him so that he could scarcely see hand before face. And through the driving snow he had glimpsed a poor woman stumbling towards him. He had hastened to help her and wrapped her in his cloak and given her a slice of his cheese to eat for she looked near starving. And when the blizzard ceased she had stood up, tall and proud, and advised him to take the path whither he was led. And while he was puzzling that out she had glowed with a light brighter than the sun so that he knew he was in the presence of the Mother of God. And as he realised that she vanished, and he saw in the air ahead of him a very young angel who flew between the high-piled banks of snow. So the shepherd followed and came to the place where our village later stood, and he settled there and prospered. The point is there was proof of the tale, for the shepherd had tried to catch hold of the angel, intending to persuade it to stay longer. The angel flew straight up to Heaven but it left one of its feathers in the shepherd's hand, and that feather we all saw with our own eyes every time we went to church, for it was kept in a case with a lid of glass at the feet of the statue. When you have seen something with your own eyes there is no doubting the truth of it.

I knelt down before the statue which was made of wood like the church and I prayed that my mother might bear her child safely and not love me less because she had a new baby and then I jumped up and ran back to the priest's domus where he and Israel were still talking.

'Did you pray well, child?' Father Hubert asked me.

'I prayed loud,' I said and both men laughed and he tossed me an apple from the table, and I caught it and ran happily down the track into the valley where the grass was lush and blossom starred and my grandmother's domus stood with the roof in need of new shingles. I liked to play in the domus because it was going to be mine one day, and I would imagine how I would sweep the floor of beaten earth and make a fire in the shallow pit and hang a pot of rabbit stew over it, and lay my pallet against the far wall and hang bunches of herbs and garlic from the rafters. I would be fourteen or fifteen then and married. In our district the girls married young but the men generally were in their twenties before they could support a family so most females were married more than once and there were always young widows for the bachelors to choose from.

I was sitting on the doorstep, munching my apple, when I heard hoofbeats and scrambled up in fright. Only rich people owned horses, and there were none such in Fromage.

The young man who came riding into the valley had black hair with scarlet ribbons wound through it and a tunic of fine fur with a garnache of red silk worn over it despite the heat of the sun. There was a peregrine falcon perched on his wrist and, as I watched, he gave a shout and launched it into the air, tipping back his head to watch it wheel and dip below the sky. I forgot to be afraid and followed the bird as it arched beneath the heavens until the sun made my eyes water and I was forced to lower them.

'Hey, girl!'

The rider had seen me and turned to ride towards me, revealing a pale, high-bridged nose with an unexpectedly full mouth. All his features were set in a long oval of a face round which the glossy black curls clustered.

'Hey, girl!' he repeated loudly. 'What are you doing here?'

'I am on my father's land,' I said.

'Your father's land? All this land belongs to us,' he said.

I knew who he was then. It was the first time I had ever seen Benet La Neige, for as I have said the family never came down into the village. He was handsome, I supposed, and most finely clad, but not very well mannered. Also ignorant, since my parents were free and had legal title to their land.

'Why don't you answer?' he demanded. 'Have you no tongue?'

'I have a tongue,' I said promptly, 'but I have nothing to say.'

'Because you admit that I am right!'

'No, you are mistaken,' I said, 'but it is rude to argue with my elders.'

'And betters,' he added.

This I would not admit so kept my mouth firmly closed and scowled up at him.

'Benet, what the devil are you about to let your falcon fly free of the lure?' another voice cried.

A tall woman, breeched like a man, with black hair streaming from beneath her veil, came riding towards us. I had only glimpsed her in the distance before but I guessed who she was, and it was hard to stand my ground for she halted only a yard from my feet, and the great horse she rode snorted alarmingly and danced a little on its hind legs.

'She says the land belongs to her father,' the young man said. His tone had become petulant.

'Who are you, brat?' she demanded, staring down at me.

'Zabillet d'Aude, if you please, my lady.' My legs shook a bit but my voice was very firm.

'She speaks true,' said Lady Petronella to the young man. 'Her parents are free. They own this land, and her grandmother — God rest her soul — had her domus there.'

'She spoke without respect,' he muttered.

'First earn respect!' she said tartly. 'You, Zabillet, what are you doing here?'

I thought it a little unfair that I should be required to account for my presence on land that belonged to our family, especially since they were the trespassers, but of course the rich had the right to go anywhere and frequently did, hunting through the corn and spoiling the harvest when the fancy took them.

'I was praying for my mother,' I said. 'She is having a baby.'

'The church is for praying,' she said, still tartly. 'Your mother will doubtless survive without your hollering to Heaven all over the place. Run home, child, and leave us in peace.'

I bobbed my head and ran off, glad to be out of reach of those hoofs though I'd never have admitted it. At the top of the fields I looked back and saw the falcon still circling below the sky and the two mounted figures, small and threatening, in the green landscape. I turned and went draggingly towards the village, hoping it would all be over by the time I reached my home. I loved my mother and it was hard to see her suffer. I had heard my father say that suffering was woman's lot because of the sin of Eve. God might be infinite, but He wasn't very fair. That was my thought, not my father's for he never had a heretical idea in his life.

As I gained the lower cobbles Guillemotte went flying past me towards the church. She was one of the best midwives in the district and when I saw the frantic fear in her face I was terrified myself and ran after her.

She was already at the door of the priest's house by the time my shorter legs had toiled up the hill, and I heard her voice raised in pleading.

'The child refuses to be born, Father. Margot pushes and pushes and nothing happens. You must come at once.'

'Is extreme unction required?' Father

Hubert was on his feet, reaching for his stole.

'No!' I flung myself forward, clinging to his legs, raising my own voice in a despairing wail.

'Child, would you have your mother go to Heaven unshriven?' he asked.

'I don't want her to go to Heaven at all yet!' I shrilled.

'It is possible the child is a breach birth,' Israel said.

'Feet first? God save us!' Guillemotte crossed herself.

'Do you know aught of child delivery?' Father Hubert asked him.

'I have seen babes who had to be turned lest they strangle themselves on the birth cord,' he said.

'Can it be done so late?' Father Hubert asked.

'There is a chance,' Israel told him.

'Then you had best come and see what you can do,' Guillemotte told him.

'Jews are forbidden to practise as physicians,' he reminded her.

'To turn a babe is scarcely practising as a physician,' Father Hubert said. 'Indeed I know of nothing that covers it in canon law.'

'If it is life or death — ' Israel hesitated, then nodded. 'First I will wash my hands and then I will come.'

'Wash your hands!' Guillemotte looked indignant. 'While you are washing your hands the two of them may die!'

'I will make haste.' He stepped calmly through the door and headed for the little brook that meandered down into the valley.

'Dear God, I trust that we are doing right,' Guillemotte muttered uneasily.

'That is all any of us do,' Father Hubert said, looking down at me, for I was clinging to him still.

'I am quite ready,' Israel said, returning from the brook with water still dripping from his hands. 'Mistress, run ahead and fetch the pepper pot from your domus. Will you come, Father Hubert?'

'To lend authority?' He prised me loose and took up his stole, draping it carefully around his neck.

As they set off, Guillemotte speeding ahead, I followed, keeping in the rear lest anyone should order me back.

Our domus was crowded with women. There were herbs burning to keep away the evil spirits, and a low wailing from the older women who crouched near the door, their hoods drawn over their faces.

'The Lord be with you,' Father Hubert said. 'Make some room now.'

He himself stood aside and waved Israel within, and I heard gasps and excited comments but I cannot recall exactly what was said. My eyes were fixed upon my mother who heaved and writhed upon the birthing stool, her mouth open but no sound emerging. Israel knelt down and began to feel about over my mother's distended stomach. Then he said sharply,

'Stand back and give us room. The

babe comes feet first with the cord about its neck.'

I was too little to see exactly what he was doing, but I heard further gasps, saw the craning of necks, as he laid his ear to my mother's belly and with his hand began to probe between her extended legs. His hand came away all bloody and he said, still sharp and with a curious authority,

'The head is free but it is too late to turn the babe. Where's the pepper?'

Guillemotte bustled in with the pot, exclaiming as she came,

'This was expensive, and the last I have until the pedlar comes again.'

Israel took the pot and held it close to my mother's face. I saw her head jerk and her glistening white face crimson, and then she gave an almighty sneeze and two tiny feet shot out from between her legs and were instantly followed by torso and head.

'A girl, by Our Lady!' Father Hubert let out the cry as he stepped to catch the infant.

'Pack the mother with sphagnum moss and lay her with her feet higher than her head once the afterbirth comes away,' Israel said. 'Mistress Guillemotte, here is your pepper.'

He rose, holding his bloodstained hands in front of him, and the women made way, some signing themselves with the cross, all of them gabbling fit to raise the roof.

'The child must be quickly baptised,' Alaizair said, 'lest she took harm from the glance of the Jew. No offence, Master Israel, but one cannot be too careful.'

'I shall baptise her as soon as her father comes,' Father Hubert said. 'A runner must fetch Jean and his sons from the hills.'

'My Bertrand will go,' Louise said.

'I'll tell him.' Another woman hurried out.

I wanted very much to get closer to my mother, to have her notice me amid all the excitement, but the women were crowding round her again and above their chatter rose the wailing of my little sister.

Then Father Hubert picked me up and strode out with Israel at his heels, and set me on my feet again on the cobbles.

'We will drink wine to celebrate,' he said. 'Come, Israel.'

He had not exactly invited me but I went anyway, trotting after them over the cobbles. When we reached the priest's house Israel went straight to the brook to wash and Father Hubert brought out the jug and three — I was glad there were three — cups, and poured wine, though less for me, and we took it to the brook's edge where the bank sloped and afforded a good view of the valley below.

'To the babe, God bless her,' Father Hubert said, and drank. We all three drank, and then the priest looked at Israel and said, 'You did well. The child might else have perished with the mother too.'

'I have seen the technique before,'

Israel said modestly.

'Our betters approach,' Father Hubert said, indicating with his head two riders coming up the hill.

'Madame La Neige?' Israel looked a question.

'With the boy, just home from his squire's training,' Father Hubert said.

I half feared, half hoped they would come right up to us, but at the last moment both veered away and vanished over the brow of the hill.

'Let us make a wish,' Israel said. 'What would you wish, my friend?'

'For a peaceful conscience,' Father Hubert said, which alarmed me for if the priest had an uneasy conscience, what chance for the rest of us? 'And you?'

'To see Jerusalem before I die,' Israel said.

'May I have a wish?' I asked.

'Of course, child.' Father Hubert looked at me kindly. 'What is your wish?'

'To be a lady,' I said, thinking of

fine horses and a peregrine falcon high in the sky.

Both men laughed and I, seated between them, wriggled my toes above the rippling water of the brook.

'I have word that two Jews have been burnt in Carcassonne,' Father Hubert said, staring down into the water.

'I too heard that rumour,' Israel said.

Both drank thoughtfully but I sensed a shadow across the sun.

'Is Carcassonne far?' I asked.

'Twenty leagues,' Father Hubert told me.

The shadow disintegrated. Twenty leagues was near the end of the world, I reckoned. Then Israel slowly upended his cup and let the last drops of wine dye the waters scarlet.

'Christ and His angels defend us,' Father Hubert said softly.

They looked at each other unsmilingly and I sat between them, sipping my wine, and wriggling my toes in the afternoon sunlight.

2

My little sister took no hurt from the odd manner of her coming into the world. From the beginning she was a good, pretty child with wide brown eyes and curly hair that had in it no tinge of red.

She was named Marie and everybody loved her. Even I loved her though she took up a lot of my mother's time. She was also the last living child my mother bore, though in the years following her birth my mother miscarried twice and had a dead daughter born three months before her time. These were not great sorrows since too many mouths to feed was never a good thing, but my mother grieved for each one. She liked babies.

In the year that my courses began I was twelve. I had prayed all through my childhood a secret prayer. It was that when my courses started my hair should lose its vivid red shade and settle down into a nice, respectable brown. But when I woke on that morning with a dull ache in my stomach and blood trickling between my thighs the long tresses of hair that hung down my back and sprang curling from my temples were as red as they had ever been. So much for prayers, I thought, and felt the stab of disillusionment.

It quickly passed for I realised that God could scarcely be expected to work miracles to please my vanity. The red hair was a cross I must bear, along with my pale skin and the pale green eyes that tilted up at the corners and made me look questioning even on the rare occasions when I was not.

Now that I was twelve my childhood was over and good riddance to it! Now I could gossip with the other women when they went down to the river to fill the buckets or harvested the corn. We talked of all manner of things. Life and death and when the pedlar was coming and if it was better to sow at new moon or full moon and whether God had created bats and rats or left that part of creation to the Evil One.

'God created everything,' Mengette said. 'Everything comes from Him.'

'But if God is good,' Arnalta said, 'why would He inflict us with vermin?'

It was a good question and the next time I saw Father Hubert I asked him. He was seated as usual at the door of his house, looking out over the mild autumn fields, as placid as ever with a cup of wine in his hands and his sandalled feet planted firmly on the earth.

'In Eden vermin did no harm,' he told me. 'Only when man sinned did evil enter into certain creatures. The evil came from man.'

'But if God created man,' I said, 'then God must have put the evil in him too.'

'Evil is contrary to the Will of God,' Father Hubert said sternly.

'Then why did God act against His own Will by putting evil into us?' I persisted.

'God gave us free will,' he said. 'Unhappily man frequently chooses evil.'

'Then why did God put it there for us to choose in the first place?' I demanded.

'Child, have you no household tasks to do!' Father Hubert said.

'They are all finished,' I said smugly. 'My mother said that I was free for the rest of the day.'

Father Hubert sighed heavily. It was clear that he wished me elsewhere.

'I cannot tell you exactly why God allowed evil to come into the world,' he said at last. 'It is a mystery.'

'The world is full of mysteries,' I observed.

'That is true.' He gave me a more kindly look. 'That is the wisest way to look at it. When a disease comes we do not enquire its cause. We seek to eradicate it.'

'And sooner or later everyone chooses the evil?'

'Except for Our Blessed Lord and His Holy Mother.'

'But if He was God He would certainly choose the good,' I argued, 'so it was no merit in Him.'

'She has you there, my friend!' Israel had come around the corner of the house and stood, his eyes bright and mocking, his head tilted a little.

'Not at all!' Father Hubert straightened himself. 'Our Blessed Lord could have refused the burden laid upon Him but did not. He resisted temptation.'

'He being God anyway?' Israel said.

'Of course.'

'Therefore, according to your reasoning,' Israel said, 'having created the world He then granted Himself the privilege of free will, set Himself a series of tests, and carried them out, knowing perfectly well that, being all good, He could not choose the bad without denying His own Nature. Not much of a contest there!'

'Perhaps there are two Gods,' I chipped in brightly. 'A good one and a bad one.'

My innocent suggestion had an unexpected effect. Father Hubert almost jumped off his stool as he cried,

'Who put that heresy in your head? Have you been talking with shepherds?'

'I don't know any shepherds,' I said.

It was quite true. In our part of the world when a lad became a shepherd he thenceforth spent his life in wandering, seldom visiting his domus again, driving his flocks through the passes sometimes as far as Aragon and Aquitaine. He returned only to choose a wife and many of them didn't even do that. They took wives from other places instead.

'It looks as if you have an embryo Cathar on your hands,' Israel said, looking amused.

I had heard of the Cathars, of course. Who had not? They had been imprisoned and burnt by the

Holy Inquisition before I was born. There had been a crusade preached against them. Now there were only a few left, moving from place to place. It was rumoured that many worked as shepherds so that they could always be on the move, hard to catch. The Cathars denied the value of the Sacrament of Penance and went about saying that Jesus was no more than a good man. That was all I knew about them, and I replied somewhat indignantly,

'I don't know any shepherds or any heretics. I get my ideas all by myself.'

'Then the Devil put them into your head,' Father Hubert said. 'Two Gods indeed. The notion is perfect rubbish!'

'An idea that many died defending,' Israel said. 'Have you never noticed how impossible it is to slay an idea? Zabillet is a bright girl.'

'Zabillet chatters too much,' Father Hubert said, frowning at me. 'There cannot be two Gods, because the Nature of God is Unity — '

'Divided into three, according to you,' Israel murmured.

'One Nature, three Persons,' Father Hubert said. 'The mystery of evil must remain a mystery.'

There were so many mysteries, I thought. How the sun and moon stayed up in the sky; where the soul went immediately after death; why an onion bulb grew up into an onion. If I lived to be forty I would never know half the questions let alone the answers.

'The trouble with you, girl,' Father Hubert said, abandoning theology, 'is that you don't have sufficient work to occupy you. Your father and brothers busy themselves on the land and your mother spoils you and allows you to idle about the place. Idle hands make mischief.'

'Would you like me to sweep out your domus?' I promptly offered.

'Certainly not, or I shall never be able to find anything again,' Father Hubert said in alarm.

'May I pick some flowers and make

a crown for the Holy Virgin?' I offered instead.

'Now that is a sensible idea,' Father Hubert said. 'Run away and make a blossom crown for the Holy Mother to wear. That will keep you occupied and gain favour with God. He loves to see His Mother honoured.'

I bobbed my head and started down into the valley. It was the dying end of the year and it would take me some time to find enough flowers to weave into a garland. The harvest had just been gathered. It was a good one and since there had been a treaty made with the English there was no danger of losing it because hordes of mercenaries rode through the district. In fact we were generally free from such annoyance since most of the fighting had been in Aquitaine and up north in France.

The lavender bushes had been plundered for the sweetening of linen when it was laid away for the winter, but there were plenty of autumn marigolds growing along the river banks with their fringed orange petals still spread wide around their furry golden centres, and there were long strands of corn that had escaped the gleaners and could be used to bind the crown. I gathered a lapful and sat down to bind them, the sun warming the nape of my neck. It was pleasant to be there and I had a virtuous feeling because I was making a crown for the Mother. God's Mother. If God created everything then He must have created His own Mother too, and how could He possibly do that before He was born? Perhaps I would ask Father Hubert about it some time. Perhaps I would not.

There were riders on the far bank. I shaded my eyes to look towards them, thinking for a moment they had come from the castle, and then seeing they were strangers with black cloaks and crosses about their necks. Priests and Dominicans at that. We all knew the distinctive black and white of the Dominicans, most of us by hearsay

41

since members of that Order hardly ever came to our district. They came to hunt out heretics and Jews.

Certainly they rode fine horses and splashed across the shallow water which was not yet swollen by the winter rains without difficulty. I stood up, clutching the marigold crown.

'Girl, come here!' The older of the two beckoned me imperiously with a hand on which gleamed a golden ring set with a sapphire.

I approached nervously, bobbing my head. The Dominican swung himself down from the saddle and looked me up and down.

'What is your name?' he asked.

'Zabillet d'Aude, — ' I hesitated, uncertain how to address him for he was much better clad than Father Hubert. Then I added politely, 'Your Holiness.'

'She thinks you the Pope, Brother Anselm!' the younger one exclaimed, laughing. He had a hard laugh and a beaky nose like a crow.

42

'There's no sin in honest error, Brother Gregory,' the older priest reproved. 'What are you doing? Have you no work that you amuse yourself like a green girl?'

'I am making a crown for Our Blessed Lady,' I said, showing him.

'For the statue of the Blessed Lady she means,' said the one called Brother Gregory.

'And anything made for Her likeness on earth is seen from Heaven above,' said Brother Anselm. 'You must not seek to confuse the child.'

'I'm not confused,' I said promptly.

'Of course not. Indeed you seem to be an intelligent girl.' Brother Anselm smiled a little wintry smile. His features were gaunt and angular, his eyes deep-set and burning as blue as the stone on his hand. 'That village yonder is — Fromage?'

I nodded.

'Your parish priest being — ?'

'Father Hubert,' I said.

'Father Hubert. I wonder if it is the

same.' He frowned slightly but there was a pleased look about his mouth. 'If so it will be good to see him again. I often wondered what became — you are all good Catholics in your village, are you?'

'I don't know if everybody is good,' I said doubtfully, 'but nobody is really bad.'

'We are here on a pastoral visit,' Brother Anselm said, remounting his horse. 'Lead the way to your priest's house then.'

Where they would find Father Hubert in friendly conversation with a Christ-killer! My face must have paled more than its normal shade for the elder priest looked down at me and said, 'There is no need to be nervous, girl. Your Father Hubert will likely be delighted to see us if he be the man I believe I know.'

There was nothing for it but to lead them across the stubbled meadows up the slope towards the long wooden building and to pray that someone else had seen our coming. Someone had. When we reached the level ground again with its downflowing stream there was only Father Hubert to greet us.

'It is indeed the man I knew!' Brother Anselm dismounted again and went forward with both hands outstretched. 'I hoped it might be. How long has it been? Ten years? You have aged.'

'So have you, my friend,' Father Hubert said. 'And prospered too.'

'As you might have done had you had the sense not to bury yourself in this backwater,' the other said.

'In fulfilment of my penance,' Father Hubert said.

'You were too hard on yourself then and you are too hard on yourself now,' Brother Anselm chided. 'Yours is an educated mind.'

'An educated mind is not always a blessing,' Father Hubert said. 'Is your companion nailed to his saddle that he sits so unbending?'

'Brother Gregory is newly tonsured and eager for the salvation of souls,'

Brother Anselm said.

'Well, let him dismount and take something to eat with me,' Father Hubert said. 'Zabillet, take the garland into the church and then run away home. You will stay the night?'

I left them to their talking and went into the church where the painted wooden statue waited. It was necessary for me to climb on a stool in order to fit on the crown, and when I had set it carefully on Her gilded hair it looked very well. I got down from the stool and admired my handiwork for a few moments and then I went back down the path and turned towards the village again.

The visitors had been seen and myself with them and I was instantly the centre of attention.

'Are they Dominicans? They look like Dominicans. Are they here to preach a crusade against the heretics? Will they stay over the night?'

I answered the barrage as well as I could until my mother said, laughing,

'Give the girl some peace, do. What's to fear when there are no heretics in this village?'

'There's Israel,' someone said.

'A Jew is not a heretic,' said Gilles who rather prided himself on his superior knowledge on account of having once been to Paris. 'A heretic is a Catholic fallen into error. A Jew is born and bred in error and so cannot be a heretic.'

'That must be a comfort when they're being burned alongside the Catholics fallen into error,' Simon said.

'God knows His own,' said Raymond piously.

'Not if Heaven's full of Catholics,' Simon argued. 'There must be thousands there already. God'd not get round them in a twelvemonth. If He exists.'

There was an appalled silence save for Guillemotte's shrill voice declaring,

'You want your mouth washing out for that, Simon d'Albret! Not exist indeed! Who made us then?'

'Your parents made you and mine

made me and theirs made them and so on back to Adam and Eve,' Simon told her.

'Ah! And who made them? Answer me that if you can!'

'Who cares? Whoever it was isn't likely to be around any longer,' he shrugged.

'I'd like to hear you say that to the Dominicans!' Raymond said.

'I'm not thinking of suicide,' Simon told him, 'and if you say anything I'll break open your head.'

'What if they ask about Israel?' someone said.

'They probably won't. Nobody ever has before,' my mother said.

'And there's no crusade against the Jews in these parts,' Guillemotte added. 'They won't ask.'

'But if they do? To lie to an Inquisitor is a mortal sin. We'd go straight to hell.'

'Perhaps we ought to murder them,' Philippe suggested. 'Before they start asking questions, I mean. What does everybody think?'

'That it's a good idea but someone would come looking for them and their horses,' Simon said.

'Then let's hope they don't ask,' Guillemotte said.

'I know what we can do,' Gilles said. 'If they ask we'll say we don't know any Christ-killers. That'll be the truth because Israel's relatives tried to save Our Lord. Father Hubert said so.'

'It's not often that I say this,' Simon declared, 'but a trip to Paris surely sharpens the mind. You have my respect, Gilles.'

'We could have crushed their heads with rocks,' Philippe said wistfully.

'You need your head crushing with a rock to get the stupid ideas out of it,' Guillemotte scolded. 'Zabillet, cover up that hair of yours and take some supper to Israel. He's in the usual place.'

The usual place where he retreated whenever strangers came was a cave hollowed out of the rocks near the spring from which the stream was born.

Obediently I covered the flames of my hair with my woollen head-square and went with her to get the cheese and bread and ale that was our standard supper. She packed them in a basket and tucked a clean cloth on top.

'Take the upper path,' she told me.

That path ran close beneath the walls of the fortress and curved into the rough ground beyond. It was not a path I often took. However one didn't argue with one's elders unless one craved a stinging ear, so I took the basket, bobbed my head and set off.

I had never been in the La Neige fortress nor seen its lower part since the high guarding walls surrounded it and around the walls was the sluggish moat that stank in summer. Behind the moat and the walls I could see the twin towers rising. It was, since I knew no other comparable, the biggest domus in the world. I thought of Lady Petronella and her grandson and their servants rattling around in it like beans in a gourd.

Benet La Neige was not at home. He had been at the Court of Aquitaine for more than a year.

In the years since I had seen him riding in the valley I had no more than glimpsed him now and then, and felt for some reason unknown to me the chill of a shadow across the sun. I followed the narrow path into the rough ground that rose up behind the castle. Here the path itself broke up into half a dozen ribbons of green trailing between the high crags and the great masses of bracken, brown and crackling now as the year sped to its close. Israel was sitting by the cave, tracing patterns on the soil with the tip of his stick.

'Mistress Guillemotte?' He glanced at the covered basket and smiled. 'Her bread is always good. Why have the priests come? Do you know?'

'On a parish visit, I think.' I gave him the basket and sat down on one of the rocks that were scattered about the entrance. 'One of them would like to find heretics, I think, but the other is an old friend of Father Hubert's. I heard him ask why Father still kept his penance here when he had an educated mind. Do you know what he was talking about?'

'A good man with an over-developed sense of guilt,' Israel said with a wry mouth. 'He has sacrificed the possibilities of a fine mind because of his exaggerated sense of sin in the belief that God will be pleased to see His gifts neglected.'

'But what did Father do that was so bad?' I asked.

'Now if he wanted the world to know wouldn't he have announced it from the pulpit?' Israel said.

'Meaning I am too young,' I said with a sigh.

'Meaning that it is his business. Look how the land is spread out before us from this high point. There are times when I climb up here even when it isn't necessary for the sheer joy of looking.'

'You said once.' I remembered, 'that your wish would be to go to Jerusalem. You can't see it from here?'

'No, but it lies at the centre of the world where the sun rises,' he told me.

'There have been crusades there.'

'Too many,' he said with quiet bitterness. 'No man can conquer Jerusalem with a sword. A man walking softly with love in his heart might find the key to the city.'

I rested my chin on my fists and gazed at him, wishing that adults would speak plain. Someone was coming towards us, striding over the rough ground as easily as if it were paved. I jumped up, my heart pounding, the scarf slipping from my head as the cloaked and breeched figure pushed through the screen of bare bramble and gained our vantage spot.

'What the devil are those two black birds of ill omen doing in Fromage?' Lady Petronella demanded.

Close to she was ancient, not far

off sixty, I reckoned, with her skin crisscrossed with a fine network of lines and more white than black in her hair. She was painted thickly with rouge, her eyes outlined with black like the Moorish people who sometimes strayed up from Aragon, and there were rings on every one of her fingers.

'They came on a parish visit,' Israel said.

'Well, I am too sick to receive visitors,' she said with a grin that showed strong, yellowing teeth.

'From what the girl tells me one of them is likely to offer you extreme unction,' Israel told her.

'Mumbo-jumbo, hocus-pocus,' she muttered settling herself upon another rock. 'When my time comes I'll choose the endura. Not that my grandson would approve. He's for the Church. So, will you stay in your cave or will you accept a lodging in my home until the black crows have all flown away?'

'I'll not put you or any of your house in danger,' Israel said.

'Be damned to that!' She laughed and I jumped again because she had a beautiful laugh as sweet and clear and rippling as the merriment of a child.

'We may both be,' Israel said mildly.

'There's no crusade preached at the moment, is there?' She looked at him sharply.

'Some men don't need a preaching,' Israel said. 'However I have an inkling these two will move on in a day or so. Zabillet here has brought me a good supper, as you see.'

Her black rimmed eyes, under hooded lids, moved to me.

'The redhead whose grandmother owned the domus in the valley,' she said. 'How old are you now, girl?'

'Twelve, my lady,' I told her.

'You have remarkable hair.' She leaned forward, taking a long strand of it in her beringed hand. 'If you are still unwed when you are fifteen come to La Neige and I will give you a post there.'

'Inside the castle?' I gaped at her.

'My maids generally work inside the building,' she said. 'Israel, do you need blankets?'

'Nothing, I thank you.'

'Independent as ever. Girl, go home. You will be missed and those black crows may add two and two and make four.'

'When I am fifteen and still unwed,' I said, rising and bobbing my head.

I did not tell her that I would not forget any more than she told me she would keep her promise. It was understood between us from the very beginning.

I went away across the rough ground and along the path that curved about the walled fortress of La Neige, and so down into the village. I thought of the Lady Petronella and of Israel and of Father Hubert and his penance for some unforgiven sin, and it seemed to me that the fine threads of all our lives were already beginning to tangle together and foreshadow some future pattern that nobody could plainly see.

And then my heart did leap into my mouth because the tall black pillar with the gleaming cross that was Brother Anselm barred my way.

'What a bustling child you are!' he said, with a down slanting smile. 'Is it not almost the *couvre-feu*?'

'That is why I hurry, sir,' I said.

'In such a hurry you forgot your basket?' He lifted a thin arched eyebrow and smiled again.

'Basket?' I said stupidly.

'Remember that it is the tiny carelessnesses that betray us,' he said. 'Run home now, girl.'

I bobbed my head and I ran. Oh, how I ran! I looked back once and saw him looking up towards the castle and then he shrugged his shoulders and began to walk another way.

3

Astonishingly during the next two years three lads made offer for me despite my red hair. It might have been the promise of my grandmother's domus that attracted them, but my shape may have had something to do with it too, for I was high of breast, narrow of waist and curved of thigh without any blemishes on my pale skin. The lads went as was proper to my father who referred them to my mother who asked me what I wanted to do. I told her that I wanted to remain unwed until I was past fifteen so that I could work at the castle. She could have told me that I was dreaming, that the Lady Petronella only employed servants from outside the district, but she left me free to choose as I pleased.

The two Dominicans had ridden away again and didn't return, but they had left a fear in the air behind them. For some time afterwards we walked warily and Father Hubert renewed his efforts to convert Israel, though without any success.

And then in the year I was fourteen there came the almost unbelievable opportunity to leave Fromage for the first time in my life and travel to Avignon. You will know, of course, that before the great schism the Papacy removed the Holy See from Rome to Avignon, and at the time of which I speak Pope Benedict the Twelfth held the keys of Peter. Nobody from our village had ever been to Avignon. It was thirty leagues off and only shepherds sometimes drove their flocks that far.

But suddenly word came that there was a new Pope who would be known as Clement the Sixth, and there were to be festivities that would last for months right up to Christmas.

'And a representative from the chief families in the village is to travel to Avignon to share in those festivities,'

Father Hubert told us all at Mass.

'But who are the chief families in the village?' Guillemotte enquired.

Father Hubert frowned at her, because in the House of the Lord women were supposed to be silent, but nothing could ever silence Guillemotte.

'Those families who have been settled in Fromage for three generations,' Father Hubert said.

'Through the maternal or paternal?' Guillemotte persisted.

'The maternal,' Father Hubert said. 'I will draw up a list and then the representatives will be chosen.'

There were murmurs since if the men were chosen there would be none left to hunt or to defend the village. If women were chosen there would be nobody to cook or take care of the babes.

'Who is going to do the choosing?' Simon enquired.

Father Hubert hesitated, and then made up his mind.

'Each of the designated families will

decide which member to send,' he announced.

'Who is going to pay for this foolishness?' Julie Beret demanded. 'How can we go jaunting off into strange lands without beggaring ourselves?'

'We shall use some of the village funds,' Father Hubert said, and left the pulpit somewhat hastily to continue the Mass.

There was always chatter after Mass, but on this day there was a babble of talk, with even those who were not three-generation families giving their opinions. Those who had a chance to go were busily finding reasons why they should or should not make the journey, and those who were not eligible either by reason of not belonging to a three-generation family or because of age, pregnancy, sickness or any other reason were equally vociferous.

There were nine families who qualified which meant that nine people would travel with Father Hubert to Avignon. I don't know what went on in the other

61

houses, but in our house my mother and father went into their bed space and talked together in low voices for a long time.

I sat by the fire and tried to see hopeful omens in the little leaping flames, because though it had never before entered my head that I might travel further than the castle, the instant Father Hubert had mentioned the scheme my horizons widened and I longed to go. Unfortunately there was little chance of it. Even if my father decided not to go there were both my elder brothers from whom to choose. Reynaud was nineteen and in love with Denise Foret, daughter of the widow in whose domus Israel lodged, and Jacques was sixteen and wanted to go as a soldier. I have not spoken of them very much, but I was never close to them. They were both tall, healthy young men who worked the land, Reynaud with enthusiasm and Jacques more reluctantly, and took scarcely any notice of me or Marie. Marie was seven and a miniature edition of my mother with her curly brown hair and merry eyes. She sat next to me, watching the fire too, as sleepy as a kitten, her brown head drooping against my arm.

At last my parents finished their muttered conversation and my father stood up and said,

'The lads and I cannot be spared from the land and your mother must stay to care for Marie. We are going to send you to Avignon, Zabillet. It is a great sacrifice for us to take this chance but you will do us credit while you are there and obey Father Hubert in all things.' For a moment I couldn't believe that I had heard aright and then I jumped up and hugged my mother so hard that she gasped and said laughingly,

'Why, anyone would think that you wanted to leave home!'

'Only for a little while,' I said quickly. 'Only to see Avignon and then come back to tell you all about it,' I protested.

'Perhaps you'll find a rich husband there,' my father said.

I smiled, saying nothing, but I wondered if that was the main reason why they had chosen me as the one to go. Were they both hoping that I would be the one to bring more riches into our domus? If so then they were not to be blamed. All parents want their children to marry well. We were to set out on the journey in late September, after the harvest was safely gathered in, and before the harsh weather swept snow and ice down from the hills.

'It will take us four days to make the journey,' Father Hubert told us. 'As the ones chosen are all healthy and strong there is no reason for any delays. We will walk by day and stay in the hostels along the way.'

It occurred to me that it would be a hard trip for the priest, but though he was bent and habitually carried a stick he was sinewy as rope and would probably outwalk us all. We set off on the appointed day, five men, four women and the priest. We wore our stout shoes and woollen cloaks and carried heavy sticks, and the men in addition had their daggers tucked into their belts, for though it was rare for pilgrims to be attacked there was no sense in taking chances.

If any in our little party had entertained any notions of impropriety along the way they were speedily disillusioned by Father Hubert before we left the village.

'We shall walk in pairs and nobody must loiter,' he ordered. 'When we reach the hostels the women will go to the women's quarters and the men to the men's. Though this is a joyous occasion we must not forget that we are going to pay honour to the new Pope. Lewdness and the singing of bawdy songs will not be encouraged.'

Everybody promptly looked as if such thoughts had never entered their heads, and I saw a grin flicker for a moment at the corners of the priest's mouth.

So we set off, with those who were

not going climbing with us to the top of the village, waving and calling and giving us last-minute instructions.

We were to stay for two days in the City of the Pope, so we would be gone for ten days. I remembered Father Hubert once saying that travel broadened the mind, and I wondered how broad my mind would be by the time we came home again.

I was walking at the end of our short procession next to Father Hubert and, as we reached the narrow path that circled the fortress of La Neige, I asked him,

'Will Lady Petronella be in Avignon?'

'I think not, child,' he said.

'Because of the endura?' I am not certain what put the question in my head, but I saw it had startled Father Hubert. He turned a sharply frowning face towards me and said,

'Where did you hear that word?'

'I'm not sure — yes, I remember now, Father. When the Dominicans came and Master Israel went up to the cave and I took some supper, Lady Petronella came from the castle to speak with him. She said that when her time came she would choose the endura. I cannot recall the conversation exactly but it seemed she was not — not altogether happy about priests,' I ended, feeling slightly uncomfortable.

'The endura is a most heathenish practice indulged in by heretics,' he said after a few moments, lowering his voice and slowing his pace so that we lagged behind the others. 'They do not believe in the grace of extreme unction. When their deaths are near they refuse all food and drink, and so hasten their deaths. They call it being hereticated and I thank God there are no more Cathars to spread their grievous errors.'

'But Lady Petronella — '

'It pleases Her Ladyship to jest,' he said heavily. 'Zabillet, you are no longer a child. In future think before you speak. With me you are safe but there are many ears in the world that would hear your innocent questions and twist them on their tongues into something vile. You understand me, girl?'

'Yes, Father,' I said meekly.

He cheered up at that, patting my arm and hastening to catch up the others, as he called in his strong voice,

'Let us sing a song in praise of the Blessed Virgin. There is nothing like a good Ave for putting spring in the steps.'

We did not, of course, sing all the way there. Our breath was often needed for climbing for in places the paths were very steep, but we sang when we reached level ground and the Holy Virgin must have enjoyed it for no rain fell and the only injury was a blister on Jeanne's heel.

It was a strange feeling to be moving further and further away from the village, from my home and parents. I wondered if I would be greatly altered when I returned. Surely I would look different in some way after seeing the city where the Pope had his palace. What astonished me more than anything was the size of the land. We walked through forest that seemed to go on for ever and climbed hills that showed us only more hills beyond when we got to the top. We walked through villages that were so like Fromage that it was as if we had come round in a circle and were at home again.

There were others on the roads, processions of pilgrims, merchants riding their mules as if they were steeds, packs of archers whistling as they swung along, solitary mendicants with their wooden begging-bowls. Oh, I had not imagined there were so many people in the world. We managed to reach a hostel before darkness fell each night, though they were crammed full of travellers and the supper provided would have curled my mother's lip in disdain.

By the third day we were beyond the foothills of the Cevennes and had got into the rhythm of walking at a steady pace, swinging our arms and taking a deep breath before we tackled the next hill. I thought it was a pity that Israel could not have come with us, but when I said as much to Father Hubert he shook his head.

'One can never be sure which way the wind is blowing,' he told me. 'Master Israel is safer where he is.'

On the fourth day when even my strong young legs had begun to ache we came to the city. To be plain with you we both heard and smelt the city before we entered its gates. In Fromage the smells were honest smells of bread and lavender and dung and sweat, but here the smell was foul and odorous with a sharp quality like steaming piss that made me want to retch. And the noise was a muttering interspersed with shrieks and cries that made several cross themselves uneasily and glance towards Father Hubert for guidance.

'We shall first find lodging,' he said,

'and then go to church.'

What he had obviously not reckoned on was that we were not the only visitors coming to gape at the sights and stare at the papal palace rising tier upon tier above the Rhone.

'Keep together! Everybody keep together now!'

Father Hubert's voice rose above the din as we trailed into the warren of narrow, cobbled streets within the gates. It was a timely warning for we were caught up and swept along in the crowds that streamed towards the squares and churches and the inns with their huge, gilded signs.

I had never seen such richly dressed folk before. Men on horseback with their cloaks spread like peacock tails over the rumps of their mounts, women reclining in curtained litters swaying by leather straps from the bowed backs of serfs, pilgrims with the cockleshell of Compostella in their hats, nuns telling their beads as they glided along, a lady with her breasts almost bare and her

71

hair dyed orange — 'Do not look,' Father Hubert cautioned us. I think he was somewhat disconcerted by it all but he took the lead and walked steadily, his expression resolute, and we struggled after him, holding on to one another for fear of getting lost in all the hubbub.

'Guide, sir priest? One groat for my services and not a better guide will you find in all of Avignon!'

A lad had run after us and was tugging at Father Hubert's cassock. A thin lad with a pocky face and the desperate merriment of the destitute in his eyes. Father Hubert paused and gave him a long, unwavering stare before he said,

'We require lodging for ten and a decent meal, boy. Then you shall have your groat.'

'Heaven bless you, sir priest,' the lad said and led us all down a series of alleys that were slimed with grease and the entrails of slaughtered beasts, and so brought us to what looked like a decent hostelry though, after speaking with the host Father Hubert emerged, shaking his head, and saying,

'It seems a decent place, but we cannot afford to stay three nights there. If we stay then we must shorten our visit by a day.'

'By Our Lady,' Guillemotte said — have I mentioned that she was with us? As well try to lock St Peter out of Heaven as leave Guillemotte out of any activity — 'By Our Lady, Father, this city makes my stomach heave! Let us make haste to see the Pope and make our purchases, and be out before we are all vomiting like dogs.'

There being general agreement, Father Hubert stepped back inside and haggled cordially for a while, and then agreed to pay for two nights' bed and board, taking the money from his boot and tossing a groat to our guide who spat upon it, bit its milled edge, and finding it sound, vanished into the stench of the alley.

We had been allotted two attics,

reached by climbing a ladder up which Guillemotte had to be hauled and shoved. There was space between the walls and the rafters so that by standing on tiptoe we could see the roofs and walls below and the people like coloured ants scurrying hither and thither. There were pallets laid on the floor and the rooms were clean. Father Hubert would have liked to go at once to church but was overruled for dusk was already stealing over the city. Perhaps he allowed himself to be persuaded because his legs were aching as much as our legs were.

So we ate a supper of meat and cheese and wine that was only slightly sour, and then wrapped ourselves in our cloaks and lay down on the pallets and slept with the noises of the city still swirling below and the stars coming out like torches to form a border of silver between walls and rafters.

'First Mass,' said Father Hubert firmly next morning, 'and then we shall go up to the palace in hopes of receiving the blessing of His Holiness.'

The streets were as crowded as the day before, but we had slept for a night and rediscovered our confidence. The stench was as bad as it had been and the noise as tumultuous. Yet there was a vitality in the narrow streets, in the cries of the hucksters presiding over their stalls at every corner that excited us all. Even Guillemotte stopped grumbling about her corns and started perking up wonderfully as we made our way to the nearest church.

That church was as noisy as the streets outside, with people gossiping so loudly one could hardly hear the droning at the altar. Only when the Sanctus bell was rung and the Host in its gleaming Monstrance elevated was there a moment's silence.

'We will go up to the Papal Palace now,' Father Hubert told us when we had struggled out into the comparatively fresh air again. 'If any get separated from the others then they must make their way to the central fountain in the piazza there and wait until the rest of us come. Now, let us walk briskly.'

And he himself set off at a brisk pace with the rest of us winding behind him. Even in the midst of this great city Father Hubert retained his air of quiet authority over us. As we neared the great edifice of walls, roofs, towers and chimneys, even his self-assurance faltered a little. He paused, looking up at the open gates beyond which lay a series of courtyards, and shook his head as he tried to get his bearings, and then we were swept along in the wake of a crowd from Lombardy to judge by their accents, and so found ourselves in the midst of a great throng.

I had never seen a palace before. You could have fitted the fortress of La Neige into one of its towers and the sun struck sparks of fire from the hundreds of windows.

'Will you just look at what we're walking on?' Guillemotte said, awed. 'Look at the tiles!'

They were patterned with flowers and leaves outlined in gold and a blue deep as a summer sky. I marvelled how they stayed so bright with all the grubby feet tramping over them, and then I saw the women on their knees patiently wiping each tiled square as the pilgrims passed.

'The Pope rides out every morning and blesses the crowds,' Father Hubert said.

There was suddenly a loud clanging sound that echoed from wall to wall and men with staves in their hands appeared from nowhere and began to force back the crowds. The huge double doors were opening and a double line of prelates wearing the wide-brimmed red hats of cardinals processed out. In their midst, riding on a white donkey, was a figure clad all in white, a skull-cap upon his head, his pleasant face turning this way and that way, his right hand raised in blessing.

There were cries from all sides of *'Viva la papa!'* People held up rosaries and tiny statuettes for blessing; several mothers struggled with their children to the forefront. One woman, holding a baby with a big head, called over and over, 'Healing, for the love of God!' The Pope, eyes kindly, in a tired face smiled and nodded in her direction. He looked lonely, I thought, among all those brilliant cardinals. Behind him came the Papal Court. It was impossible to distinguish clergy from laity for all were magnificently attired, their sleeves slashed and fur-edged, feathers in their hats, troops of little dogs with silver collars trotting after them, and some distance behind a young woman in a litter, her kohl-rimmed eyes the only part of her that showed above a golden veil.

'Who is the lady?' I shook Father Hubert's sleeve impatiently.

'She is intellectual companion to His Holiness,' he told me.

'Oh,' I said.

'Looks more like his — ' Guillemotte began.

'*Viva la papa!* God bless the Vicar of Christ!' Father Hubert cried with great enthusiasm. And we all yelled loudly and waved, sinking to our knees as the tired, kind eyes briefly glanced our way.

'I've gone all of a tremble,' Jeanne gasped. 'To see him so near, so near and looking so human!'

'Father, we must buy a relic for the church at home,' Guillemotte reminded him.

There were relics being sold everywhere. In the corners of the courtyards booths were being hastily erected and the cries of hucksters mingled with the paean of praise.

'Two groats for a bottle of the Holy Mother's breast milk! Only a groat for a sliver of wood from the True Cross! Only come and see the henna with which the Blessed Virgin dyed Her sacred hair!'

'There is so much choice,' Father Hubert said uncertainly.

'We already have the Archangel's

Feather,' Julian reminded him.

We began to move from stall to stall, arguing over the various relics offered for sale. One of the arrows that killed St Sebastian found favour for a while; others preferred a piece of the cloak that St Martin gave to the beggar; Guillemotte spoke up loudly for a scrap of parchment that was part of the marriage contract between the Holy Virgin and St Joseph.

'A tress of the hair of the Magdalen, sir priest? Three groats. Cheap for you and your party since I see you have travelled far,' a stout man coaxed.

The tress was as red as my own and tied with a green ribbon.

'Is it genuine?' Father Hubert asked with a worried air. 'I have heard that people are often cheated.'

'This tress was cut when the Magdalen landed in Provence after the Crucifixion,' the other assured him.

'It is certainly true that the Magdalen came into France,' Father Hubert admitted. 'Three groats seem rather a lot. What do you all think?' He looked round at us.

'Buy it, Father. It can go in the glass case with the Feather,' Jeanne urged.

'You want feathers, sir priest?' The man at the next stall joined in. 'I have a feather that the Blessed Michael tore from Lucifer when they fought together.'

'I'll have nothing that belonged to the Devil in my church,' Father Hubert said with a frown. 'I think we will take the Magdalen's hair.'

He counted out the money carefully and put the tress in his cassock. There was a general murmur of approval since now that had been accomplished we could enjoy ourselves with an easy conscience. And there was much to enjoy. Every street had its taverns and pastry shops, every square its jonglers and minstrels and decorated archways. Everywhere the bells pealed and the visitors frolicked. It was a fine thing to be in a city, and such a city!

The day fled by on wings and

as the first torches were lit so the dancing began, the music shrilling, feet pounding, wine both red and white streaming into the conduits. Of course we all got separated. There was no helping it. I saw Guillemotte whirled into the measure by a merry-faced lad half her age which might explain why she wasn't protesting too loudly; Jeanne speedily found a tavern where she could rest her blistered feet and slake her thirst; Gilles disappeared entirely and was not seen by anybody until the next morning when he turned up with a satisfied grin on his face, complaining of a headache.

' 'Tis more likely to be your cock that's aching,' Father Hubert told him. 'Ten Aves and pray God you haven't caught the pox.'

But that was the next morning. That evening, having given up hope of keeping with the rest, I went wandering with a pleasant sense of independence, now grabbed and joining the dance, then breaking away to munch at a slice of eel pie someone had thrust into my hand. I found myself by chance and not by design at the central fountain in the piazza, and saw Father Hubert seated on a stone bench in the shadow of the looming gargoyles, his head bent, his hands laid upward on his lap.

'I found my way here, Father,' I said virtuously, but he raised his head wearily, looking at me in the light of the flaring torches as if I were a stranger, and said,

'I ought not to have come. I am unworthy to visit the City of the Pope. I hoped that this time all would go well, but nothing ever does. I have lost the hair of the Magdalen and my poor people are cheated of their relic.'

'You couldn't have lost it!' My voice rose in dismay. 'It must be somewhere about you.'

'There are pickpockets in the crowd,' he said groaningly. 'Three groats flung away and nothing to show! What am I going to tell everybody?'

'Father, you need tell them nothing,'

I said, sitting down next to him, my words tumbling out with the brilliant idea the Holy Virgin had just popped into my head. 'Take your knife and cut a tress of my hair. If you take it from underneath nobody will see and 'tis the same colour as the hair you bought.'

'Child, that's downright cheating,' he said.

'It was the Holy Virgin put it into my mind,' I said modestly.

'Did She?' He turned his head and looked at me attentively. 'Are you certain?'

'I am sure of it, Father,' I said truthfully. 'I can't imagine getting the idea all by myself.'

'I don't know. You are sometimes alarmingly bright for a female,' he said moodily. 'If I could believe that you were led here — from underneath, you say?'

I pulled back my hood and turned my back, heard him sigh and murmur an Ave and then part the long strands of my hair, and cut through one of them with his knife.

'It is exactly the same shade,' I reassured him, pulling my hood up again, and turning. Father Hubert was smoothing the tress between his fingers. There was a gentleness in his fingers that had nothing to do with me or my hair, or the Magdalen's hair either. It was as if his hand, moving backwards in time, stroked the hair of some other woman. The impression lasted only a moment. Then he put the tress into his cassock, saying briskly,

'The green ribbon never belonged to the Magdalen in the first place. Thank you, Zabillet. You and I will keep this to ourselves. Who knows but faith may sanctify the hair? Come, we will take a little walk and then return to wait for the others. You will not mind my company? I did promise your mother to keep an eye on you.'

'No, I shall enjoy your company the way I always do,' I assured him.

'Ah, the day is coming when you will prefer the companionship of a lad instead of an old cleric,' he said.

'Not I, Father,' I said confidently. 'I am going to work at La Neige when I am fifteen, and I may not wed until I am twenty years old.'

'Perhaps you have a religious vocation?' he said hopefully.

'No, I don't think so, Father,' I said firmly, lest he let the notion lodge in his head.

'Well, the Holy Virgin knows Her own,' Father Hubert said. 'Now we shall eat a tart together, and watch the dancing, and then we shall meet up with the others, please God.'

He bought two apple tarts that were thick with honey and we squeezed into a narrow space in the angle of two walls where two large stones did duty as seats and watched the people go by, reeling, laughing, dancing, spinning colour into the torchlit night.

'Father, why did you say that nothing would go right because you were not worthy?' I ventured to ask.

'Because it is true, child.' His voice

was sad again and I was sorry that I had asked.

'I think you are a good man,' I said encouragingly. 'I have heard people say you are one of the best pastors they ever knew.'

'People see the deeds of men,' he said, 'but God sees the heart. He sees the hidden sins, the guilt that refuses to be shriven which is itself another sin. Believe me, Zabillet, but only men who have done evil know the extent of their sinning. Their outer goodness is but the cloak that covers corruption. And these are gloomy words for a holiday! Look, there is a magician. Shall we go and watch him? I dearly love to watch a magician.'

'Be careful he does not cause the hair to vanish,' I said, and Father Hubert put his hand, the one not holding the apple pie, into his cassock and I held on to his sleeve and we went to watch the magician who was indeed most wonderful. He held up a stick and behold! it was a bunch of coloured paper flowers, and then he turned the flowers upside down and wine flowed from them, and then he turned them another way and a white dove flew out of them and perched on his head.

'I hope there is no sin in our watching this,' Father Hubert murmured uneasily at one point. 'I fear that he learned his magic from the Devil.'

'Didn't you tell us that Moses turned his stick into a serpent?' I said.

'Yes, but that was a diff — oh, he has just now taken an egg from that man's ear! Oh, that is one of the cleverest things I ever saw. Bravo, Master Magician!'

His gloom had gone and was not to return even when it rained on the way home and Guillemotte told us all that she had heard a tale of folk who went off on a jaunt and returned to find they had been away for a hundred years and their village was crumbled into dust and all their loved ones sunk into the earth. She told it so well that two or three of the men decided to run ahead, just to make sure, but before they had gone far we saw the neighbours hastening to meet us, and then there was such exclaiming and embracing and kneeling before the relic.

I suppose it is still there, under the glass with the Archangel's Feather, and only two people ever knew that it hadn't come from the head of the Magdalen at all. Indeed I believe that Father Hubert convinced himself that he had dreamed its loss and the cutting of a tress from my hair. Except for the sin that still troubled his soul he generally saw what he wanted to see. I have always seen everything and so had less peace of mind. Unless the Holy Virgin did take pity and make a real substitution out of pity for our belief. Sometimes, Sister, I like to think that She did. Like the magician, you know, with the flowers and the egg and the dove. Nothing is impossible.

4

Although I was glad to be at home again that visit to Avignon awakened something in me — a craving for colour and bustle and movement and the unexpected. Very little in Fromage was unexpected. Day followed day and season succeeded season with little change. I wanted something different to happen but I couldn't think what it might turn out to be.

'You are restless,' my mother said. 'At your age I too became restless and then your father came to lodge in the village and when I laid eyes on him my restlessness ceased and soon after we were married.'

I know she expected that the same thing would happen for me, but I was not as sure as she. For one thing I had no particular desire to marry since once a girl was married it was all work and childbearing even if one were fortunate enough to have a loving husband. And I still strained forward to the time when I would go up to La Neige and remind Lady Petronella of the bargain we had made.

That was a particularly harsh winter with the snow falling early and lingering long. It was as if the village itself had resented our journey to Avignon and so took steps to keep us all close to home for a while. The harvest had been a plentiful one and plenty of game had been killed for the winter so there was no danger of famine, and wood for the fires had been cut and the roofs strengthened against storms, so there was little to be done but sit it out until spring. There lay the difference between me and the rest. They were content to spend their winter going from one house to the next to drink wine and gossip while the children made slides and played on them, but I looked around at the sharp peaks of the icy hills and saw them as prison walls holding us all fast.

There was nothing to prevent me from walking up into the hills beyond the fortress, provided I was careful not to stray so far that the light dwindled before I came down into the village again. I often took my stick and put on my high boots and walked up that way, towards the cave where Israel had hidden when the Dominicans came. At this end of the year it was hung with icicles and there was a thin rime of frost on the surface of the stream. When the sun shone the icicles looked like jewels.

It was a few days after Christmastide. In our village we always ate pork at Christmas and drank spiced wine after we had been to the Nativity Mass. On the day after the Nativity all was turned topsy-turvy in accordance with custom.

The church was stripped of its Chalice and Monstrance, and the statue of the Holy Virgin covered lest She be shocked at the goings on.

One of the men — this year it had been Gilles — was chosen to be priest for the day, and dressed himself in Father Hubert's old cassock inside out, and we all flocked into the church behind him singing the rudest songs that we knew, and rushing to the altar where there were jugs of wine and dice and strings of sausages and black puddings for the taking while Gilles offered a 'mass', with a slice of beetroot for the 'Host', and obscene gestures that had every member of his congregation in fits of hysterical laughter. It was a custom that Israel tried in vain to understand.

'How can you make a mock of your faith?' he always demanded at this time of year.

'It's a poor faith that cannot take a little mockery,' Father Hubert said.

He himself did not join in, but kept an eye on proceedings lest they get out of hand. Usually they didn't, since despite the fun we all knew that the mess had to be cleaned up and the mock priest sobered up and helped back into his own clothes before midnight struck on the big gong that Father Hubert kept for the purpose. I noticed that sometimes midnight came fairly early on the day after Christmastide.

Yes, it was a few days after that when I went out into the crisp white snow and walked up the path that curved around the fortress. It was a beautiful day and yet I was the only person who was out in it. Even the young folk were huddled by the fires, holding their hands to the flames that rose from the crackling wood.

The water in the moat was frozen so that the surface was smooth and milky white with no trace of the refuse that lay at its bottom. Everything looked more beautiful in the winter as if the cold had cleansed everything and revealed its purity.

I walked round the path to where the frozen spring hung its jewelled icicles and stopped dead, seeing two figures stooping there to crack the ice so they could get at the water below. They were strangers and I felt a very natural thrill of alarm, for in this season not even pedlars travelled.

One of the strangers was elderly, in his late thirties, with a dark blue cloak and hood. The other was just a boy, not much older than myself. I stood staring at him and he straightened up and stared back at me.

There are moments that are engraved on the heart, that for some reason remain in the mind as if, by some curious alchemy, one was both present in the scene and at the same time apart and witnessing. So I stood and looked at the lad and, at the same time, I saw us both, a small girl in her fifteenth year with the hood slipping back from her unbound red hair and the lad with hair so light that it looked silvery, and unexpectedly dark eyes in a lean, brown face.

That was the first time I saw Alain Berger though I did not, then, know his name, nor anything about him at all. I only know that we stared at each other for a moment that lasted for many years, and in that instant I knew how the long length of him would feel pressed against me and the demanding caress of his mouth and the scent of his skin.

'What is it, Alain?'

The older man turned, wiping his mouth with the corner of his cloak, and saw me. Clearly they were not robbers or soldiers come to rampage. It was polite to greet them.

'God give you welcome,' I said.

'What village is down there?' the older man asked.

'Fromage, sir. My name is Zabillet d'Aude,' I volunteered.

'Bernard Vital,' he said, 'and my companion is Alain Berger. I am travelling to Narbonne.' He was a poor man then, to be walking south with no mule or donkey. Yet he looked neat and clean enough with stout boots and a stouter stick with which he had been splintering the ice.

'I don't know how far it is to Narbonne,' I said. 'You will find shelter in the village.'

'Who is headman in Fromage?' he asked.

I hesitated, for we had never chosen an official headman.

'Father Hubert, I suppose,' I said at last.

'A priest.' He spoke the word flatly.

'He is a very good man,' I hastened to assure him.

'No doubt,' said Bernard Vital.

Taking another look at him I said, struck by an idea,

'Excuse me, sir, but are you a Cathar?'

'Haven't they told you that all the Cathars were burned long since?' he replied. 'We are all good Catholics now.'

'It is only that the demoiselle who lives in the fortress will choose the endura when she is dying,' I said.

'Has she a name, this demoiselle?' he demanded.

'Lady Petronella La Neige,' I said.

'La Neige? La Neige? The name stirs echoes.' He gave me a long steady look. 'Is she at home?'

'I think so, sir. She very seldom comes down into the village,' I said.

'Then I will beg a night's shelter.' He turned to the lad, holding out his hand as if they were equals though the boy was more shabbily dressed. 'I thank you for your company, Master Alain. Now you had best get back to your flock before they stray.'

He went off down the path without another glance at me, sliding a little on the snow. The boy watched him and then turned and looked at me.

'Zabillet?' he said. 'That's a pretty name. How old are you?'

'I will be fifteen in May,' I told him. 'You?'

'About seventeen. Do you live at Fromage?'

I nodded.

'I am from Cahors,' he told me. 'You are a shepherd?'

'Yes. The snow blocked the pass and I was for turning back when I met with the *parfait*.'

That, I knew, was what they called the good Cathars who went from place to place, trying to persuade men to live simple, virtuous lives. They ate no meat and did not commit adultery.

'Are you a heretic?' I asked.

'I am not anything,' he said and smiled at me, displaying strong white teeth. 'I am Alain Berger, a shepherd.'

We both knew already that he was more than that in my life as I was more than just a village girl in his life. It was as if we had lived our brief span incomplete without knowing it, and now were completed each by the other, with no word spoken.

'Even shepherds stay at home when it snows,' I said.

'Not this shepherd!' He laughed. 'I never could bear to sit by the fire like an old man. When winter comes I seek the sweet pastures under the snow for my flock.'

'You have your own flock?' I was impressed since few men could afford their own flocks until they were in their twenties.

'Since last year when my father died,' he told me. 'My mother and I share the sheep.'

I had never thought of shepherds as having mothers and fathers. To me they had all the wonder of strange and independent beings who came and went like the wind. They formed a community outside the community in which more settled people lived.

'Are you a heretic?' he asked me now.

'No, of course not. I am a good Catholic,' I told him.

'But you knew about the heretic demoiselle.'

'Perhaps she is not a heretic any longer,' I said, feeling a twinge of alarm. Perhaps it had not been very wise to open my mouth on the subject.

'I hope she gives the good man shelter for the night,' he said. 'I will wait until it is clear that he has not been turned away.'

'I will wait too,' I said.

He nodded as if something had been decided between us and pulled off the blanket he wore about his shoulders over his cloak, spreading it over a stone with an air of gallantry.

'We can sit down if you like,' he said.

'You are not seeking shelter?' I looked at him hopefully as we sat down together on the rock.

'I must get back to my sheep. Do you have a husband?'

'No.' I felt the colour rising in my face.

'Why not?' he wanted to know.

'When I am fifteen I am going to work in the castle,' I said. 'I don't wish to take a husband yet.'

'Have you a family?' he asked.

'Yes, of course. A mother and father, two older brothers and a little sister. Have you any brothers and sisters?'

'There is only my mother.' He shot

me a glance from beneath eyelashes as black and curling as a girl's and said, 'I have no wife either.'

'At seventeen you are too young to take a wife,' I said.

'In the spring I will be nearer eighteen. It looks as if Master Vital found shelter.'

'And you must be getting back to your sheep.'

'I will come again in spring,' he said and rose.

I rose too so that he could take up the blanket again. He threw it about his shoulders and stood looking at me.

'Your hair makes a fire against the snow,' he said. 'Until spring then.'

It was settled between us at that instant, not just his returning but everything that came after. All settled with no more words spoken as he turned and went away, striding over the smooth whiteness and leaving the imprint of his boots like wounds upon the snow. When he had gone I made my own way down past the rugged mass of the fortress walls and the blue white ice of the moat. I had reached the gates when an imperious voice called to me. Wrapped in wolfskins the Lady Petronella stood on the drawbridge and called to me.

'You sent the traveller here to seek lodging. Why here?'

'It seemed to me to be the right place, my lady,' I said, going as near as I dared to the edge of the moat.

'And now you are running back to gossip in the village, eh?'

'I don't gossip, my lady — or at least not very much,' I protested.

'See that you don't gossip about my visitors,' she said. 'You hear me, Zabillet?'

'What visitors?' I asked, and she let out her high, silvery laugh, saying,

'You are so sharp you'll cut yourself one day. Run along now.'

I bobbed, but lingered to enquire,

'Please, my lady, how do you recall my name?'

'Because you told it to me, dolt — ah,

you are right. Lords and ladies do not usually recall the names of peasants. Well, I have a marvellous memory, but most peasants look the same to me, like herds of cattle that sway anonymously through the landscape. You are different. You have a face, Zabillet, and hair that the Devil stroked on a witching night. Run away now.'

I ran, not sure if I liked the reference to the Devil, but thinking to myself that it was true. I had a face. I would never go anonymously through the landscape.

The snows lingered a few days longer and then began very slowly and reluctantly to drip into water again. Those who had grumbled at the ice grumbled now at the mud. Later in the year they would find fault with the drought. They grumbled about everything to prove to themselves they were alive, I supposed.

Sometimes I thought of Alain Berger. Does it sound strange to say that I didn't miss him or waste time that was meant for sleeping in craving his company? I was happy enough at that stage of my life to make pictures in my mind of how it would be, and it never occurred to me that he might break his promise. I knew that he would not.

With the melting of the ice the passes were open again and travellers began to move more freely up and down the land. Pilgrims passed through Fromage on their way to Compostella; pedlars came with the spices that we couldn't grow in the high country; soldiers came — fortunately not many — for they usually drank the place dry and got into fights before they moved on.

There were rumours that the English had broken the treaty with France and that their king was planning another campaign.

'Which means prices will shoot up everywhere to match the taxes,' my father said. In truth the campaigns made little difference to us but they formed a good topic of argument, with some believing the Auverge should stand with France and others declaring that as the Duchy of Aquitaine belonged to the English monarch anyway then he might as well take the rest.

'As we shall never lay eyes on the king what matter who it be?' Simon said, glaring round belligerently.

'We never thought we'd ever see the Pope,' Jean Petit said, 'but we did. Who knows what will happen?'

'One trip to Avignon and he is polishing up his manners for Court,' Gilles said, giving Jean Petit an almighty shove that tipped him off the bench on to the floor.

'If there is war again I shall go and fight,' my brother Jacques said.

His announcement brought a sudden silence. In that silence I saw my father frown and my brother frown back defiantly. At seventeen Jacques was as tall and as broad as he was, his habitual expression louring and sulky. He would have been handsome else.

'No lad of mine,' Father said at last,

heavily, 'shall make carrion for the dogs of war.'

'I shall earn my spurs,' Jacques said.

'By valour on the field I dare say!' Father threw back his head and gave a loud, uneasy laugh. Jacques got up and walked away and I uncurled myself from the stool in the corner and went after him. I was not close to my brothers, but there had been something in Jacques' face that reminded me of the way I sometimes felt.

'What do you want?' He turned as I caught him up in the street outside.

'Do you really mean to go to war?' I asked.

'One day. Sooner or later.' He nodded his dark head fiercely at me. 'Father and Reynaud can easily work the land between them without my help. I don't want to spend all my life in this hole.'

'But you would need money with which to buy weapons and boots and a horse,' I said.

'I know what I would need,' he said

irritably. 'I don't need a fool of a girl to tell me.'

'Perhaps you could hire yourself out as a shepherd and earn money that way?' I suggested.

'I know nothing and care less about sheep,' he said, still irritable. 'What is it to you, anyway, whether I go or stay?'

'Because I too would like to travel,' I said.

'You already did. You went to Avignon.'

There was such resentment in his tone that I was surprised. He had said nothing when I had been the one chosen.

'Father only sent me because I am not so useful at home,' I said placatingly. 'And Avignon is not as far as some other places, Rome or Jerusalem or Babylon.'

'Can you imagine going to those cities?' His face lit up and his irritability vanished. 'Oh, Zabillet, I would give anything! And to fight like a real man instead of bending over a hoe or dragging a plough — I would sell my soul — '

'No, you would not,' I interrupted hastily, crossing myself. 'You might give a great deal but not your soul.'

'You think not?' He gave me a mocking little grin. 'We shall see, sister. We shall see. One day, I swear, you will see me mounted on a horse in fine clothes.'

'And you shall see me dressed like a lady,' I countered.

'For which you would sell your soul?'

'No, of course not. Jacques, does Reynaud ever wish to leave Fromage?'

'Why should he when he has his Denise Foret to snuggle up with when Mother's back is turned?'

'If the Widow Foret catches them she'll force a marriage.'

'Which would please Reynaud very much. I think he is hoping that the girl becomes pregnant so that he can be married young and have his own domus.'

'Then he is fornicating,' I said, feeling rather shocked.

'So's half the village,' Jacques said, 'but you'd not notice unless you fell over them. If you sometimes used your eyes instead of wandering off by yourself or spending hours talking to those two old men you'd know what was going on.'

'Father Hubert and Master Israel talk about interesting subjects,' I said defensively.

'And fill your head with nonsense. Sooner or later you'll find yourself spread eagled beneath some lad — '

'Not while I've still got fists!'

'Or are you thinking of becoming a nun? They have fine times with the monks if truth were told.'

'You don't know any nuns so how can you say that?'

'I know what I know.' He laid a finger down the side of his nose and went off whistling. Perhaps Jacques had a face too, I mused, wanting more than he had, seeking something. In that he was more like me than were Reynaud and Marie. Reynaud could not conceive of an existence outside Fromage and Marie was sweetly content in our little world.

'Do you think that Jacques will ever go for a soldier?' I asked Father Hubert the next time that I sat with him and Israel.

'I think he will do what he wants to do,' Father Hubert said. 'He has a stubborn mouth.'

'If the Pope preaches a crusade then he can volunteer for that,' I said.

'If nobody ever volunteered for a crusade then the world would be a happier place,' Israel remarked.

'You want the holy places to remain in the hands of the Saracens?' Father Hubert looked shocked.

'As long as they exist still and are not profaned then it makes no matter in whose hands they are,' Israel said. 'You know yourself that crusades are only excuses for killing other human beings and picking up plenty of loot along the way. And of course the brave crusaders practise a little bloodletting along the way by killing any Jews or Moslems or Cathars they can find.'

'I defend the spirit but cannot always condone the practice,' Father Hubert agreed.

'Which is not to say that I would not give much to see Jerusalem one day,' Israel said with a little sigh.

'Have you relatives there?' I asked foolishly.

Father Hubert gave me a kick, but Israel answered with only a faint shadow on his face.

'I have no relatives anywhere, child. Or to be more exact no blood relatives with whom I can claim cousinship. My wife and two sons were killed in the last pogrom when I was away on business. When I returned our little community was dead and our houses still smoking. I came south.'

'And fell among friends,' said Father Hubert. 'Not that I can approve of your theology, but I pray constantly that one day your eyes will be opened to the Faith. I only worry that I am not, by reason of my great sin, the worthy one who can convert you.'

'If I were ever to contemplate for a second the sheer madness of apostasy then you, my good friend, would be the only man who could lead me to it,' Israel said, 'but don't hope for it.' I wondered again what great sin so weighed upon the priest's soul. I might have asked, but I had had one kick already.

And then I forgot about the secrets of others because spring was coming, heralded by the flowers that made a tapestry of the hills.

You who now have chimneys in your walls cannot conceive of the joy of being able to light your fire out of doors or, if within, to be able to leave door and shutters open to waft the smoke away. There would be fresh meat now and fish jumping in the swollen streams and the fields to be sown with the grain we would harvest in autumn. And for me this spring was special. Alain Berger was coming back. I felt it in my bones, heard his footsteps singing in my heart. I told myself that I would know the moment he was approaching, but it wasn't quite like that. Nothing ever is. To tell you the truth I went every day to the foothills behind the castle and waited there in the hope of meeting him. Of course I could not go without some excuse for now it was spring and winter idleness was over, so I appointed myself, wood gatherer. It was not easy to find wood on the higher ground where the trees were sparse, but I contrived to fill a basket with twigs and sticks every day and when there was no wood I gathered moss and herbs, and astonished my mother who had always regarded me as a bit of a dreamer by the eagerness with which I went off on my search every day.

And in the end, when April was shrilling the advent of May, he came at last, driving his sheep before him, the blanket thrown over his shoulders.

I had not forgotten the silvery fair hair or the dark eyes in the tanned face. Even after the long winter his skin was still sun-touched. I wish I had the skill to make a picture of him so that you could see what I have carried since in my mind. His nose was straight and his mouth wide with the lower lip full and tender and his chin square, obstinately square, and when he smiled his face lit into something I wanted to go on looking at for a long time. He smiled when he saw me, not in surprise but in confirmation, and drew level with me, holding out his hand and taking mine as naturally as if we had been clasping hands for all our lives instead of touching for the first time.

'If I graze my sheep down in the valley will anyone give me lodging?' he asked.

'In the valley is my grandmother's domus,' I told him. 'It is to be mine one day. I am sure my mother will allow you to shelter there.'

'Not if we walk down into the village holding hands,' he said.

We unclasped hands with sheepish grins at each other. We had still not kissed. It was, for the moment, sufficient simply that we were together. I think we both felt that the kissing would do no more than set a seal on what had been begun long before we even met.

You are frowning, Sister, because in saying that I come close to heresy, close to the Cathar belief that men are born many times into this world as they struggle upward towards perfection. Well, much of what they believed struck me when I thought about it in after years as foolish, a reaction against the corruption of the times, but in that belief I consider they had grasped a truth. Alain Berger and I knew each other at a level above ordinary everyday conventions.

My mother was spinning at the door of our house as we came down the street and she looked up in the quick, shy way of a mother who sees her daughter with a strange young man. I was glad that she didn't look her thirty-five years, for her pretty skin and sound teeth prefigured what I would look like at that age, and I wanted Alain to admire her.

'Master Berger needs a place to lodge for a while,' I said. 'May he stay in Grandmother's domus?'

'It needs repair,' she said doubtfully.

'I can repair it in return for my board there,' Alain said.

'And what of rent?'

My mother might be pretty but she was no soft fool.

'These sheep,' he said, indicating them, 'are my own and my mother's. When I leave I will give you one for your cooking-pot.'

'Where are you from? Of what family?'

'From Cahors. My name is Alain. My mother is a widow, pretty like yourself.' He gave her a smile that brought an answering smile to her own lips.

'I see no reason why you should not stay,' she said. 'Until you cook for yourself you may eat your suppers with us.'

'Shall I show him the domus?' I asked eagerly.

'I need you to help me in the house,' she said. 'I will call Reynaud to help him settle in. When he has taken a meal with us will be time enough for you to go parading about.'

She did not ask me then or later how we had met or fallen into conversation. She must have sensed the bond that tied us together, but being a decent woman hoped to safeguard my reputation.

'Thank you, Mistress,' said Alain and swung past with his flock towards the valley.

'That's a comely lad,' was all she said when he had gone.

'He is nearly eighteen,' I said.

'Well, now that he is come perhaps you'll forget all this nonsense about working at La Neige,' she said.

'I can work there still,' I protested.

'Not if you go out for wood and come home with moonbeams in your basket,' she said.

'I'll go and get some wood now,' I said, blushing at the empty basket.

'Child, we have enough wood for the next three winters,' she told me, pinching my cheek. 'Go and call Reynaud and then come and help me. Lads eat a lot and we must feed our guest lest he stray like a sheep.'

And she laughed and pinched my cheek again, but gently as mothers do.

5

That same evening Alain came up to eat his supper with us and the rest of us sat and fired questions at him in the custom of our village. Where had he been born? What had his father died of? How large was his mother's domus? How much wealth did the sheep bring him? He answered in the same brisk fashion. Born in Cahors; father died of the coughing sickness two years before; the domus was small but there was a vineyard attached to it which brought his mother more revenue; he did well enough out of his flocks.

'And you are not a heretic?' my mother said.

'No, but I don't often go to Mass,' Alain told her.

'Who would if their wives didn't nag them to it?' my father said, laughing.

'But you must make yourself known

to the priest,' my mother said. 'Zabillet will take you to him in the morning. Will your sheep stray?'

'Not while there is grass in the valley,' Alain said, and soon after bade us good night.

I slept well that night with the knowledge that Alain lay in my grandmother's domus, and at dawn I was awake, tugging a comb through the red tangles of my hair and wiping my face and hands with a wet cloth. My mother raised her eyebrows as she noticed the efforts I was making, but she only said,

'Take the lad some bread and an apple to break his fast.'

I took them and fairly flew down the long street towards the fields with their fringes of woodland. I went so fast that though several neighbours hailed me I merely waved my hand and went on without stopping. It was so seldom that a shepherd came into Fromage that they wanted to discuss the event.

Alain was out in the field and he

came to greet me, thanking me for the food, sinking his teeth into bread and apple. He had been gently reared, for he wiped his hands on the dew-damp grass before he took the food, and he took small bites and chewed with closed mouth.

'I am to take you to Father Hubert,' I said. 'He will have said his Mass by now.'

He never broke the rule that a priest must say Mass once every day and though nobody bothered to attend save on Sundays and feast days we all felt more secure knowing he was doing his duty.

'Am I to be jealous of this priest?' Alain asked, smiling at me.

'He's an old man,' I assured him, 'and a holy one. He lives chaste.'

'Then that will be a rare sight to see,' said Alain and, taking me by the shoulders, kissed me for the first time. His lips tasted of the apple he had just eaten. Then we walked together up the path towards the church and the priest's house. As I expected he had finished Mass and was seated by Israel on the banks of the stream, both of them deep in conversation as usual. He broke off as he saw us approach, shading his eyes with his hand.

'Father Hubert, this is Alain Berger who has come to lodge in Fromage with his sheep,' I said, and paused, seeing that Father Hubert's face had suddenly gone stiff and still, every line on it etched sharp in the morning sun.

'Good day to you, Father,' Alain said politely, including Israel in his nod.

It was Israel who spoke first for Father Hubert was still staring.

'Welcome, Master Alain. I am Israel and — '

'Where are you from? Of what village?' Father Hubert interrupted. His voice was harsher than I had ever heard it.

'From Cahors, sir priest,' Alain said.

'Cahors.' He drew out the two syllables into a long groan. 'Your mother's name? What is your mother's name?'

'Yolande,' Alain said.

'Then there is no mistake.' Father Hubert spoke with a flat finality, and heaved a deep sigh.

'Something ails you, Father?' I said in concern.

'No, child, I am well enough,' he said, 'but my past comes walking towards me out of the sunrise. Your mother has hair of that fair shade?'

'It is white now, sir priest,' Alain said. He looked puzzled.

'Your father is — ?'

'He was Claud Berger. He died of the coughing sickness the summer before last.'

'Yolande wed then,' Father Hubert said. It was not a question. He spoke as if to himself.

'My friend,' said Israel. There was a faint warning note in his tone.

'I knew your mother years ago,' Father Hubert said at last. 'She had hair so silver-gold that once seen it could never be forgotten. Was her marriage a happy one?'

'As happy as most,' Alain said. 'You know Cahors then?'

'Knew it long since,' Father Hubert said. 'Your mother was chief ornament of the village.'

'She is comely still,' said Alain.

'And you are come to stay here in Fromage? Well, the Audes are good people. They will give you fair lodging. You are a good Catholic, I trust?'

'A Catholic certainly,' Alain said.

'I have something to do in the church,' Father Hubert said, rising abruptly. 'See to your sheep, lad. Zabillet.'

He nodded to us both and went towards the church in a hurried, agitated manner as if there were Saracens within.

'And I must finish planting the Widow Foret's crop or my life will not be worth a shekel,' Israel said.

As we went down into the valley again Alain said to me, 'Do you think that priest is my blood father?'

'I think so,' I said carefully. 'He often speaks of an old sin that weighs upon his soul, and forbids him peace of mind.'

'I think so too,' Alain said. 'My father was a good man, but I never felt any particular closeness to him. I favour my mother in feature. Yes, I think it very likely.'

'Does it trouble you?' I ventured.

'To be a priest's bastard? No, why should it? Does it trouble you?'

'No,' I said. 'It was not your sin.'

'Then I will save up and buy my legitimacy from the Bishop,' Alain said.

'Will Father Hubert admit he is your blood father?'

'I hope so, but he will have to do penance for it.'

'I believe he has done the penance already,' I said, remembering the visit of Brother Anselm and Brother Gregory. 'There would be no further penance surely. You will have to talk with him.'

'First I will save up for the legitimacy,' Alain said. 'Then you and I will be married.'

'Oh,' I said.

'Our children will be beautiful,' he told me. 'Also legitimate.'

Thus we made our plans and set the bounds in a couple of sentences. Really important matters are usually arranged thus.

Word that Alain Berger was the priest's bastard spread like dandelion fluff on the wind. I am not certain how. Neither Alain nor I spoke of it and I am sure Israel did not, but we were not fools in Fromage. Father Hubert might be ashamed of his sin but he was openly proud of the result. He never lost an opportunity to praise Alain for the good care he took of his flock, for the way he mended the roof and fitted door and shutters to my grandam's domus, for the respectful manner he behaved in church — as if the rest of the congregation were in the habit of cavorting during the

Eucharist. It was clear from every word and glance that Alain meant much to him, and since Father Hubert was no sodomite — neither was Alain for that matter — it was plain that Alain Berger was his by-blow. Nothing was said out loud, but there were whispers and a few smiles, in Simon's case a smile of relief, 'For,' said he, 'if a saintly man like Father Hubert has a bastard there's hope for the rest of us.'

That spring and early summer were jewelled seasons. In France the great nobles quarrelled over who ought to sit upon the throne of France, for King Philip was only nephew to the late monarch whereas King Edward of England was his grandson.

'Through his mother, Isabella de Valois,' Gilles said, who, on account of having been to Paris, was intimately acquainted with the private doings of royalty.

'Inheritance cannot come through a woman,' Jean Petit objected.

'It does in Fromage,' Guillemotte said.

'There is no royalty in Fromage,' Simon reminded her.

'Then why is Aquitaine in the fief of the English king?' Gilles demanded. 'Because he inherited that domain through Eleanora of Aquitaine. Answer me that.'

'He inherited it before the law about women was passed,' Jean Petit said smugly.

Gilles hit him and they wrestled together for a while.

In the middle of summer Father Hubert and Alain went off together to the nearest ecclesiastical court at Carcassonne. Everybody knew why they had gone. Alain had sold one of his sheep and had sufficient with which to purchase his legitimacy. They would be away for five days and I remembered how as a child I had fancied that twenty leagues led almost to the end of the world. While they were gone I was to watch Alain's sheep to take care they didn't stray, though they showed little inclination to do so, but grazed placidly on the high summer grass.

'When I return we will make definite plans,' Alain said.

The knowledge that his mother had once lain with a priest had not discomposed him in the least. In that he showed himself more mature than I was, for though I was not close to my father it would have upset me terribly to learn he was not my father at all. Alain, however, had a wide and lovely tolerance of human frailty. In that, at least, he resembled his blood father.

I was thinking of these plans he had mentioned as I sat in the meadow with one eye on the slow-moving sheep, their thick winter fleeces summer-clipped. He meant formal betrothal which, as you know, is as legal as marriage provided the vow be given before two witnesses. That we loved each other and were destined to be together were two facts I would never have thought of questioning, but even when he had purchased his legitimacy Alain must still save carefully so that he could make offer for me, and since my parents were not likely to allow me to bond myself to a shepherd then he would have to settle to farming, and we would both be trapped in Fromage. He was accustomed to travelling with his flock and I craved a wider view of the world, but wedlock and custom would hold us fast.

On the highway beyond the meadow I discerned movement and stood up in order to see better. There were people riding up to La Neige, bypassing our narrow village street and taking the broader track. I could see fluttering pennants and hear laughter and the clip-clop of hooves. I ran towards the wide ditch that separated fields from highway. Lady Petronella was entertaining guests, it seemed. Rich guests, but then only the rich would be invited to La Neige. I stood at the edge of the ditch and watched them pass, the armed escort gleaming with the weight of breastplates and helmets and pikes, the young gentlemen clustering together on their caparisoned steeds, with their hair curling to their shoulders and their cloaks vividly hued in scarlet, azure and emerald, the girls mounted too with their long skirts split to reveal limbs clad in parti-coloured tights. There were two curtained litters swaying between the horses. They would carry the elderly ladies in the party.

Two of the riders rode a little apart from the rest. The lady was two or three years older than I was, with her face masked against the sun and huge blue eyes revealed above the mask. Even from a distance of yards one could see the blue, rimmed on her eyelids with gold paint. Her gown was deep azure sprinkled with gold stars and its sleeves were double sleeves, the inner sleeves close to the arm, outer sleeves lined with silver and gold and edged with fur attached at the elbow and falling to the stirrups. Her golden hair was braided in a caul set with sparkling stones and her legs were enclosed in azure hose. She must be a princess at least, I thought, and was suddenly conscious of my own tumbling hair, my faded skirt that barely reached my ankles, my bare feet, for in summer most of the young folk went shoeless. Then I noticed the man riding with her. I had heard scarcely anything in recent years of Benet La Neige, Lady Petronella's grandson. He spent much time at Court, it was said, and was popular there. It was also said he had a castle in Lorraine where he preferred to spend much of his time but this I took to be exaggeration. Now I saw him again, the pale oval face within the curling black hair, the haughty features. His eyes were not dark as might have been expected but pale, cold grey. They stared at me now and then, without saying a word of greeting, and I was sure he recognised me, he turned his head towards the azureclad lady and said something too low for me to catch. It must have amused her and its subject must have been myself since she glanced over in my direction and then laughed. Then they spurred onward to catch up the others and there were only spirals of dust rising from the highway. Have you ever known envy, Sister? I knew it then, tasted the bile of it. I wanted a dress with hanging sleeves and a caul of little sparkling stones to hold my hair. I wanted to ride on a fine horse and visit the fortress as an honoured guest.

That was when I made up my mind that Alain and I were not going to settle in Fromage or even in Cahors. We would go to the city. In the city there was money to be made. I was not sure how it might be done, but that was something I could think about later. What mattered was that neither Alain nor I should limit our horizons.

There was the usual gossip in the village, of course, about the guests at La Neige. From what I gathered, since I didn't volunteer that I had seen the cavalcade, though my account would have interested everybody, the Foix cousins had come to stay, and that Anne Foix was confidently expected to marry Benet La Neige. Well, she was welcome to him. I had no liking for cold grey eyes and a sarcastic smile.

Father Hubert and Alain returned on the fifth day, having drawn ever closer during their journey. Though the truth about their relationship was not openly spoken it was accepted in the way most things are accepted in our parts.

'And I have my legitimacy,' Alain told me the first chance we had to be alone. 'Father Hubert went and spoke with the Bishop and afterwards the Secretary gave me my legitimacy.'

'Was it expensive?' I asked.

'All that I had saved from last season,' Alain said wryly. 'To be honest, I'd not have worried about the matter, since I only just found out that I was a bastard, but our children must be of a legitimate line.'

'Perhaps we ought to get married before we think of children,' I said, smiling at his earnest tone.

'And when will that be?' He took my hands eagerly.

'Not yet,' I said, wishing that I could say otherwise. 'Alain, we have no money.'

'I still have my flock and you have your grandmother's domus,' he said. 'By next season I will have made more money from the sale of the fleeces.'

'Then let us wait,' I urged. 'Alain, so many people rush into wedlock when they are poor. I would have us both comfortable before we marry. There is no law that says we have to live in Fromage.'

'My mother would welcome you in Cahors,' he said.

'And we will visit her there,' I said quickly, 'but, oh Alain, you don't want to be a shepherd all your life, do you?'

'It's a good independent life,' he said, frowning slightly.

'With the husband away half the year while the wife sits in the domus? That isn't my notion of marriage.'

'What is your notion of marriage?' he asked.

'For husband and wife to be together all the year as friends and lovers,' I said.

'For you I would turn farmer,' he said generously.

'Wouldn't you like to live in a city?' I ventured.

'Not much. Where would I keep my sheep?'

'You just said that you would give up shepherding.'

'To farm. I'd be happy if you were content.'

'Contentment is for the old,' I said impatiently. 'Alain, if we wait a year or two and save up hard we could buy a — a tavern. Not here and not in a great city, but there must be some little cities where there are taverns for sale, and then we could save up and buy some land on the edge of the city and build a house on it.'

'You have worked it all out, I see.'

He was smiling but I sensed that he was not altogether pleased.

'We are both so young, Alain,' I pleaded. 'Let's not dig a hole for ourselves and sit in it for the rest of our lives. If we wait two or three years then we will both have money for I too will save. I shall be paid when I go to work at the castle, and I will save every livre.'

'And I shall keep my flock for a year or two yet?' He sounded as if some slight compensation for the delay had just loomed on his horizon.

'Between here and Cahors, and so see both your mother and me turn and turn about,' I said.

'And you will be working at the castle? Will they pay you well?'

'I don't know,' I said honestly. 'But I can learn things if I am there. I can learn how to do fine sewing and how to dance and play the lute.'

'Zabillet, you are going to work there,' he broke in. 'The demoiselle hasn't offered to adopt you, has she?'

'No, of course not, but I will be able to see others doing these things and imitate them,' I said obstinately.

Alain stared at me for a moment and then his dark eyes glowed and he caught me in his arms, saying as he kissed me,

'I think I am going to marry a woman with ambition. But we must be betrothed.'

'Do you think I am going to run away with someone else?' I teased.

'I don't know.' He was serious all at once, tracing the contours of my face with his finger. 'I met you and knew even before we spoke how it would be with us, but sometimes I have the strange feeling that at the core of you, under the fiery hair and the grass-green eyes and the loving voice, there is ice which may melt or pierce me to the heart. I am afraid of losing you.'

'You'll not lose me and I'll never pierce you to the heart,' I said.

'Then I shall ask your parents formally,' he told me.

He did so the next day when he came up for supper. Though he had built a fire hollow in the old domus and might have cooked for himself my mother was of the opinion that a lad needed food prepared by a woman and insisted that he join us.

He made his request very formally.

'My name is Alain Berger and I have a certificate of legitimacy and a flock of sheep, also the inheritance of my mother's domus and vineyard in Cahors when she dies, though I pray that won't be soon. In two or three years I will have money saved, but I wish to be troth plighted to your daughter, Zabillet.'

'I thought there was something in the wind.' My father winked at my mother. To my surprise she did not wink back but ceased her ladling out of soup and sat down on the bench by the table.

'Zabillet is going to work at La Neige,' she said, 'and you are a shepherd.'

'I will sell my flock and settle when

we are full married,' he assured her.

'How does Zabillet feel?' She glanced towards me.

'The girl's in love,' my father said. 'How should she feel?'

'Love is something else,' my mother said. 'Zabillet, do you want a formal betrothal? I tell you both frankly that I am against it, very much against it. To be betrothed is to be neither married nor unmarried. Suppose, God forbid, something should happen to Alain and you were not told of it? Then you would have to wait seven years in order to presume him dead and be released from your vow. It is better to wait and marry when you can be full partners.' I was so much in agreement with her that I was nodding my head long before she finished.

'It is not because of — my father?' Alain said.

'Lord, no!' My mother laughed, laying her hand on his arm. 'We knew that Father Hubert buried himself in this tiny parish in fulfilment of some penance or other. I am only relieved that his sin was not murder. No, Master Alain, you are the lad I would have chosen for my girl, but wait a while before you bind yourselves. What private promises you choose to make is up to you, of course.'

I knew Alain was disappointed and I was sorry for that. I was even a little disappointed myself for I truly loved him and part of me wanted nothing more than to be his wife and bear his children, but the other part of me yearned towards that moated fortress on the hill where I could learn skills that would enable both Alain and me to better ourselves. Young as I was I knew that until the two parts of myself were united I wouldn't be the wife that Alain deserved to have. Perhaps he was right and at the core of me was a sliver of ice. If so then I take no blame for it because we have a duty to be true to our own natures.

Meanwhile the summer danced itself

into autumn and Alain prepared to leave. He was going back to Cahors to see his mother and to sell his flock, now grown plump and with their fleece thickening as the wind chilled.

'With the money I will buy more sheep,' he said, 'and sell those after another year, and then we shall wed.'

'We shall be closer to it anyway,' I temporised, and kissed him hard before he could question my insistence on delay.

Had he done so I could not have answered because I didn't understand the reason myself. When he left it was like seeing all my happiness vanish over the brow of the hill. He would return in the spring and lodge in my grandmother's domus again. The winter that loomed ahead seemed longer than any winter I had known.

'You will tell your mother about Father Hubert?' I asked.

He shook his fair head.

'I love my mother and also the memory of the man I knew as my father. Why should I cause her pain by raking over what happened in the past?'

'You are a good man, Alain,' I said. 'Sound and sweet like a summer apple before the wasps sting it and turn it brown.'

'You will make me vain,' he said, laughing, and linked my arm with his as we went up the hill, the sheep following as tame as house cats, until we reached the fortress where our ways would part until spring.

'Love me until I come again,' Alain said, and kissed me hard and briefly, imprinting his mouth on mine.

I stood and watched him until he had disappeared over the brow of the hill. Then I turned to the high gate at the end of the drawbridge. A tall figure was framed in the opening, veil fluttering in the breeze.

I could have walked away, gone down again into the village. I have wondered a thousand times how matters would have turned out if I had done that. But I set my foot on the drawbridge and went instead towards those stone walls and that tall figure.

6

Lady Petronella stepped aside so that I could walk through the open gate past the gears and pulleys that, in times of siege, would raise the drawbridge, and so enter an enclosed courtyard with steps leading both up and down. I stood politely and waited while she looked me up and down.

'You have come to work for me then.' It was not a question.

'Yes, my lady.'

'Come then.' She turned and swept up the staircase. She was not wearing breeches this time, but a skirt with a train under a loose tunic cut like a man's *cote-hardie*. We entered a small space with decorated screens ahead of us and more steps winding up at the left and right.

Lady Petronella went past the steps and through the gap between the screens. I would have liked to pause to look at the brightly painted birds and flowers that decorated the screens, but I told myself there would be time for that later and followed her into the hall. Jesu! that was a splendid hall. Oh, I have seen ones more magnificent since. I dare say if I were to go back to La Neige now it might seem quite modest, but to my fifteen-year-old eyes it looked as grand as the palace of the Pope at Avignon. It rose up through two storeys with windows set high in the stone slanting rectangles of light on the rush-strewn floor. At one end was a dais with table and benches and a high carved chair. I knew without being told that it was the demoiselle's chair. There were shields and weapons on the walls, and a central hearth with four sides to hold the wood and a chimney that rose up and went straight to the roof.

There were several girls clustered round the hearths, talking and laughing. I had seen one or two of them before and knew them to be the maidservants that Lady Petronella had brought with her from her native Lorraine. They were neatly clad with their hair braided and shoes on their feet. When they saw us come in they ceased their chatter and bobbed curtseys.

'Zabillet is come to serve me,' my employer said. 'She is very ignorant but will learn fast.'

'Welcome, Zabillet, I am Marie.' One of the girls, evidently a kind of leader, held out her hand in a friendly fashion. 'These are Laura, Claude and Miguette. What work is she to do, Madame?'

'Let her learn from you and make herself useful where she can,' Lady Petronella said, and swept out again.

'You will need proper clothes,' Marie said, looking me over critically but not in an unfriendly manner. 'Come and see what fits you.'

She went back through the screens and began to mount the right-hand staircase. I followed her, wondering how long it would take to accustom myself to the spiralling stone, and the others followed after. They seemed nice girls though their accents were, at first, difficult for me to follow since they spoke French and not the local dialect. I had to listen carefully and I fancy they had the same trouble when I spoke though they were too polite to say.

The two staircases led to the tiny rooms that were built at varying levels about the hall. Each chamber had a slit of a window and a narrow landing that led from the steps before the stairs twisted up again to the level above. In some were pallets and a stool, in others huge chests bolted to the floors, in others there were privies with narrow shafts that led down into the moat. Now I understood why it stank so in hot weather.

At the top of the fortress the two staircases met at each end of a narrow gallery which struck me as the pleasantest place I'd seen so far, with sweet rushes strewn over the floors and embroidered cloths hung all over the walls. We had to be directly over the hall for the stone chimney rose up through the middle of the gallery, effectively dividing it into two. One half was furnished with stools and looms and spinning-wheels, the other contained a high bed piled with cushions and hung with velvet and several of the big brassbound trunks.

'Her Ladyship sleeps there,' Marie told me, nodding towards the bed. 'The rest of us sleep in the little chambers save when guests are here and then we lay down pallets in the solar.' She nodded towards the other half of the gallery.

The other girls were opening one of the great trunks and pulling out garments. The one called Laura said, 'You must have two shifts and two gowns, a cloak and shoes, also hose and a veil. These will look well.'

She held up one of bright green and another of slate blue. One of them, the green one, had hanging sleeves and my mouth watered with desire.

'Isn't it against the sumptuary laws for an untitled girl to wear green?' I ventured.

'Foh! Lady Petronella doesn't give a fig for the sumptuary laws,' Claude said scornfully.

'Try it on,' urged the one called Miguette.

Oh, but it suited me and fitted too, outlining my breasts and flowing to my feet in a way no gown ever had before. I looked down, smoothing the fine cloth with my hands.

'It was made for you!' Marie exclaimed. 'Now we must have girdle and veil. Claude, bring your comb. Zabillet must not walk round with her head looking as if she had just been pulled through a thornbush.'

I bridled at that but she meant no rudeness. They were all pleasant girls, daughters from the families of merchants in Lorraine and happy enough to be serving Her Ladyship since in due course when they had learned genteel ways she had promised to make good marriages for them. When my hair had been smoothed into a caul — it was too thick to plait — they fixed the veil on my head. It was attached to a circlet of stiff green ribbon and I felt like a queen wearing a crown as I stood before them.

'She will do very well,' Lady Petronella said, coming through a curtained archway beyond the bed. I wondered if she had been watching us all the time.

'She will need better shoes,' Marie said.

'I will have the shoemaker make a pair,' Lady Petronella said. 'Do you ride, child?'

'No, my lady,' I said.

'Sew, weave, spin, make lace, embroider?'

'Not the last two, my lady.'

'Dance, sing, play upon the clavichord?'

I shook my head.

'Then your days are going to be fully occupied,' she said, smiling slightly.

'The others will help you and you will learn very fast. Now you may go down to your parents and take them this.' She handed me a small leather bag tied at the neck. It clinked slightly.

'My lady?' I looked up at the thickly painted face, the wise eyes.

'Come back then and we will begin your employment,' she said, explaining nothing.

I went down the winding steps, holding the bag in one hand, and my skirt in the other lest I trip, and walked through to the drawbridge gate. I walked more slowly than I usually did, with my head up. Changing one's garments makes a great difference to one's carriage and gait. When I reached my home I was already followed by a crowd of neighbours who'd rushed out to see my finery and exclaim that I must have come into a fortune or sold my soul to the devils.

'Not a bit of it!' my mother cried indignantly, rushing out with the rest.

'She has gone to work at La Neige. Why, Lady Petronella knows a good girl when she sees one.'

But she was as incredulous as the rest, bustling me within, shutting the door in the faces of the others as she demanded,

'Zabillet, what are you doing in that fine dress? And bright green! You have no title. What is Lady Petronella about?'

'She has employed me as serving maid,' I said breathlessly, 'and she sends you this.'

I gave her the bag and she loosened the cords gingerly and poured the little heap of coins out on the table.

'This is generous,' she said and her eyes shone for a moment. Then she hastily gathered the coins up again and dropped them back into the bag. 'Zabillet, we'll not tell your father of this payment but keep it between us. This will help towards your dowry. Now where can I — take it to Israel. He will keep it safe for you.'

'I will come very often to see you,' I said. 'It is very grand at La Neige, but I will come often.'

'Work well for Lady Petronella,' my mother counselled. 'Come when you can. Now go and find Israel.'

She kissed me and traced a cross on my brow and came out with me, scolding her neighbours loudly as I went towards the church.

'For heaven's sake, anyone would think that I had kept my daughter in rags until now. She is working at the castle now and must needs dress decently.'

I found Israel as usual talking with Father Hubert. It was odd that an unbeliever should spend so much of his time near a church, but I suspect that if the conversation had been good he'd have sat happily enough anywhere. Both elderly men looked up as I approached, and Israel cried,

'Zabillet has turned into a fine lady, I declare!'

'I am working at La Neige,' I said.

'Working? In that gown, with your hair in a caul and a veil like a lady?' Father Hubert said. 'What kind of work, pray?'

'Serving-maid to the demoiselle,' I said.

'You will continue to visit us, I hope?' Israel said. 'You will not become too grand for us now, will you?'

'I shall never become grand,' I said, but even then I wasn't sure if I was telling the truth.

'And you will not neglect to attend Mass?' Father Hubert persisted.

'No, Father. I suppose Lady Petronella has her own priest.' I frowned slightly as I spoke, for I had not been shown the chapel yet at La Neige, and if there was a family chaplain surely he and Father Hubert would have been on visiting terms.

'Lady Petronella is from a heretic line,' he said slowly. 'Long ago she was even questioned by the Church Commission, but no action was taken against her. She attends Mass, she tells

156

me, when she visits the Court, and since her servants are from Lorraine then there is little I can do to persuade them to the Communion rail. But I baptised you, my child, and I have some authority over you, so you must tell the demoiselle that I expect to see you in my church at least twelve times a year.'

'Yes, Father,' I said, 'I will ask her if I can visit my mother on the same days.'

'I will walk down with you,' Israel said, rising. 'It's a long time since I appeared in public with a beautiful lady.'

'Don't turn her head with flattery,' Father Hubert said anxiously. 'Zabillet has always been a good, modest child. What she learns at the castle will help her to order her household well when she weds Alain.'

What he was really saying, I realised, was that he feared I would forget Alain and think myself too fine for a shepherd. It was a foolish notion, and I answered him confidently,

'I shall be a good wife to Alain when the time comes.'

'As he will be good husband to you,' he said, and motioned me to kneel that he might bless me.

'If you knelt down, my friend, I would be glad to give you blessing too,' he said to Israel.

'Good Father, I am too stiff in the joints to go bobbing up and down as Christians do,' he said. 'But your good wishes you may bestow upon me at any time. Come, Zabillet.'

He took my hand and we went down the track together. As soon as a curve in the land hid us from the church above I stopped and gave him the bag.

'My mother wishes you to keep it safe for me,' I said.

'Lady Petronella gave you this — for wages?'

'I think so, but I haven't set my mark to any agreement yet,' I said.

'If she asks you to do so then bring

the agreement to me first,' he ordered. 'One should set one's mark to nothing until it has been read. But as to my keeping this, where is safe? The Widow Foret is a good woman but she has a large amount of curiosity.'

'My grandmother's domus!' I beamed as I thought of it. 'Nobody ever goes there except Alain, and he uses the house only to sleep in. There are loose stones at the back of the domus. Could you not put the bag behind them and cement it in or something?'

'Indeed I could.' He gave me a questioning glance. 'You don't want Alain to know?'

'I want it to be a surprise for him when we marry,' I said.

'Then I will do it. Hurry back to La Neige now. You will come and tell me about all the fine doings there when you come into the village?'

'I promise,' I said, and he watched me as I went off in my grand green dress, turning more than once to wave to him as if I were travelling a hundred miles and not only to the top of the hill. Yet, in a way, I was travelling more than a hundred miles. I was entering a world that was different from anything I had known before.

There were more rules of conduct than I had ever heard about in my entire life. Not only did Lady Petronella expect her servants to take a bath all over four times a year, but she insisted they washed their hands before meals and combed their hair every day. As for manners, the list of don'ts was as long as the calendar of saints. We must not wipe our fingers on the tablecloth, nor blow our noses on our sleeves, nor breathe into people's faces unless we had chewed mint or fennel to sweeten our mouths. We must curtsey to our elders and betters, not a bob of the head but with knees bent and our skirts spread wide. We must cut up our food small and chew it with our mouths closed; we must wipe ourselves with a piece of cloth when we shat and pissed; we must hold in our belches and not interrupt when others were in conversation.

There was scarcely enough time in the day to complete our tasks. Hours were spent tracing patterns on velvet and silk that had to be embroidered with fine thread; more hours were spent, by me at any rate, in practising music, in learning to ride without clinging frantically to the saddle, in counting time under one's breath as one danced, in remembering which dish must be served on bended knee.

Lady Petronella was old fashioned in some respects. She considered reading and writing were a waste of time for girls, weakening the memory and putting ideas in their heads — an opinion not in the least mitigated by the fact that she could both read and write.

'Not only must you be accomplished in society but you must learn how to rule your house well,' she was given to saying. 'You cannot hope to gain the respect of your servants unless you can perform their work better than they can.'

So two or three hours a day were given to learning how to add up accounts, how to baste a duck or a chicken so that the skin crisped evenly on the spit, how to scrub dishes with sand before washing them, how to measure out the spices for hippocras wine, and remove grease stains from clothes with chicken feathers dipped in hot water. Some of those things I had already learned from my mother and was both quicker and neater than my companions, but of the finer accomplishments I had known little or nothing, and I applied myself most assiduously to my lessons, thinking of the day when Alain would be able to say to his customers at the tavern,

'My good wife will entertain you with a song now or a tune upon the clavichord, whichever you prefer, sirs.'

When winter closed in life at La Neige was much warmer and more comfortable than in the domus. The stone walls and the heavy shutters banished the freezing wind and the hearths leapt with flame from morning to night. Yet there had been compensations at home that I missed here. Since Benet La Neige and his friends were in Lorraine — yes, Lady Petronella did indeed have another castle there — there were many tiny rooms where we could sleep separate. I had never slept in a whole room by myself before, and I missed the cuddly warmth of my little sister and the companionable snoring of my father and brothers.

I kept my promise and went down into the village every month to attend church and see my mother. Lady Petronella gave her permission with a smile that was edged with scorn. In her own household she was more openly heretic, not seeking to bend us to her will but letting fly little darts that made me, at least, look with a fresh eye at what I believed.

'A good Jew or Moslem is worth more to God than a bad Christian,' was one of her axioms. Another was, 'If Saint Peter truly holds the keys of the kingdom he may decide to let in the *parfaits* and shut out the Pope.'

The *parfaits* were the good Christians, in her view, who abstained from fornication and the eating of flesh, and had no patience with the sale of relics or pardons or indulgences. There were very few of them left since the great crusade against them, but there were some still, moving under cover from place to place, carrying with them their belief that Heaven was gained by good deeds and not by faith.

Of all this I said nothing when I saw Father Hubert, but it seemed to me that, on the whole, people needed their images and sacraments as shields against the great dark that lay beyond. It seems so to me still.

In the spring Alain came again with a larger flock of sheep. I had been watching out for him for days and when I saw him, afar off, coming over the hills, I flew to Lady Petronella to ask her leave to go and meet him.

'The shepherd lad who wishes to marry you? Of course you may go,' she said, 'but not running out like a mad thing. One of the men will fetch him in and you shall greet him in the hall as befits a modest maid. Hurry and tidy your hair, child.'

Thus it fell out that instead of running to fling myself into his arms I stood in the hall at La Neige and curtseyed low with my skirts held wide and my hair combed into a caul and half hidden by a filmy veil.

'My lady.' He pulled off his cap and bowed to Lady Petronella in the polite way he always had.

'Master Alain, here is Mistress Zabillet, quite well and very happy to see you,' Lady Petronella said. 'I will leave you to talk awhile for you'll not want an old woman to make a third. Zabillet, give your friend a beaker of wine. She spiced it herself, Master Alain, and it tastes very good indeed.'

She swept out in her majestic way

and Alain gaped after her for a moment and then looked about the hall which, for once, was deserted save for ourselves.

'This is a fine place,' he said, awed. 'The lady must be very rich.'

'Never mind the lady. Look at me!' I commanded.

'I'm looking,' he said in an equally awed tone. 'Lord, Zabillet, you are the loveliest thing I've ever seen.'

'If you touch me I won't break,' I said breathlessly.

'Not here,' he said. 'I am not at ease in this place. It is so large, so rich.'

'Drink some of my spiced wine,' I offered, hiding my disappointment. 'That will put you at your ease.'

I poured out the wine and gave him a beakerful and as he drank his dark eyes glowed at me over the rim and he seemed to relax a trifle, though he still hadn't embraced me.

'Did you get a good price for your flock?' I asked.

'An excellent one,' he said. 'I gave

one third to my mother and with the rest I bought more sheep. And you?'

I nearly told him about the bag of coins now safely cemented into the back wall of the domus, but that was to be a surprise when the time came to be married, so I said merely,

'I am learning a great deal here. Lady Petronella gives us instruction in music and dancing and embroidery.'

'And the spicing of wine,' he said, draining the beaker and giving me his familiar grin.

'Also the dressing of geese and ducks and the marinating of fish and a thousand other things,' I told him proudly. 'I shall be the most accomplished wife you ever saw.'

'When?' he asked.

'Oh, in a year or two,' I said. 'We shall begin our married lives together in prosperity.'

'A year or two?' For an instant a queer expression flashed into his face but it was gone before I could analyse it. Then he gave a little shrug and

167

moved towards me, taking my hands and bending to kiss the tips of my fingers.

'I come into the village every month,' I told him. 'I will ask for extra time while you are here so that we can see each other as often as possible. She is very kind and will allow it, I am sure.'

'Then I shall have to buy myself a new tunic and hose,' he said, 'that I might be fit to escort such a fine young lady.'

He was smiling and his eyes were loving, but it wasn't quite the same. The year before he would have caught me up in his arms and whirled me round and kissed me soundly upon the mouth.

'I have missed you,' I said. 'Alain, I have missed you so much.'

'I can imagine,' he said, and there was a certain dryness in his tone.

'It's true,' I said crossly. 'I have been looking out for you for weeks. Don't you believe me?'

'Yes, my sweetheart,' he said then. 'I believe you. When will you come into the village again?'

'I will try to get leave to come tomorrow. You will stay in the domus?'

'And eat supper with your family.' He nodded. 'Are they all well?'

'Reynaud is to be wed in the summer to Denise Foret,' I told him, 'and Jacques is still full of ambitions to be a warrior with a fine horse, and Marie is my mother grown young again. Did you tell your mother about us?'

'I told her that I had met the most beautiful girl in the world the last time I went to Cahors,' he said. 'This time I told her that I was planning to marry the most beautiful girl in the world. When I return to Cahors I will be able to tell her that my future wife is also a very accomplished young lady who lives in a fine castle.'

'As serving maid,' I said quickly.

'As serving maid,' he agreed and again the odd expression flashed into his face.

I might have asked what troubled him, but at that moment Lady Petronella swept back in. 'Forgive me, but it is time for you to help Mistress Claude with the lace,' she said. 'You must give your friend leave to go now before his sheep stray into the moat. Tomorrow I shall not have need of you in the morning so you are free to go down into the village. It is good to see you smile so happily, Zabillet. I fear she has quite lost her heart to her shepherd.'

Laughing, she bustled him out without seeming to bustle him anywhere. When she returned she was still chuckling.

'What a handsome lad and what a stink of sheep!' she cried. 'We must burn rosemary to get rid of the stench. See to it, my dear, will you?'

'Will it be allowed for me to take extra time to see Master Alain?' I asked.

'He is your friend — sweetheart, I should say,' Lady Petronella said. 'Of course you must find time to see him. It is the mark of a young lady to be considerate of others.'

She patted my shoulder and went out, leaving me in the great hall. She had called me a young lady when, in truth, I was only a serving maid, but the new description flattered my vanity, and when I sniffed it did indeed seem that there was a lingering smell of sheep in that grand, splendid hall.

7

After the initial meeting Alain and I were at ease together once more. We went to the domus where I helped him build his cook fire and sweep out the winter muck and when the tasks were done we sat close and talked of the future, of my becoming a wife of whom he might be proud. 'I was always proud of you,' he said, but I ignored that and showed him how gracefully I could step a measure and how frequently I hit on the true note when I sang.

When I went back to La Neige he walked with me, but after that first time he did not again enter. He always left me at the drawbridge and turned away before I had entered the gate. I had the feeling that he never much liked to talk of my life there, yet Lady Petronella was very punctilious about giving me sufficient time off to see Alain.

I can tell, Sister, from the look on your face even though you do not voice it that you are curious as to whether Alain and I ever consummated our love during that spring and summer. The answer is that we did not. All peasants are not brute beasts who couple without thought. Alain respected my decision to wait and I was still in that stage of loving when the touch of a hand is worth an entire consummation. You blush and shake your head. Well, perhaps you have never known it, dedicated to God in childhood as you were.

Where was I? Ah, yes, it was the summer of thirteen forty-six and in that July the war was raging again. The English had mounted another campaign and were burning, looting and killing their way north of us. At Crécy they won a fine victory — fine for them but not so good for the many French knights who were killed or taken prisoner. In the southern lands we heard the tidings of these battles and marvelled that Edward of England should dare to attack Philip de Valois and marvelled more that he should win the field, though God be thanked the enemy didn't enter Paris but swung away to Calais and besieged it.

'If only I could go,' my brother, Jacques, sighed, pulling up grass with his hand and shredding it in his restless fingers. 'Father declares that foot soldiers are regarded as less than the weapons they carry or the beasts they tend, but how can I ever hope to be a knight?'

'You could turn shepherd and save your money,' I suggested.

'Sheep are not to my liking,' he said moodily, still plucking the grass. 'Reynaud thinks me stupid to want something different but you understand, don't you, sister?'

I nodded, thinking that in that sense he and I were alike.

'If Father paid me wages,' he went on, 'then I could save something, get a start.'

'But he will not?' Alain looked at him.

'What father gives his son a wage unless that son be preparing to wed?' Jacques said.

It was true. Sons worked as unpaid labourers until they expressed a desire to marry and so could demand wages. Where a man had very little land his sons usually hired themselves out to wealthier farmers or took themselves off as shepherds.

'So find a wife,' Alain said, smiling at me.

'And be trapped here for ever? Soldiers take many women, not just one wife — not that that is why I want to be a soldier,' he added hastily.

I eyed my brother with speculation, wondering how many girls he had already tumbled. At eighteen he was good-looking in a heavy way, his eyes brooding under thick brows. Reynaud was different, his features sharper, his manner quiet and pleasant, yet I guessed that he too had tenacity.

He had chosen Denise Foret as bride when they were both scarce children and never altered his mind.

'I wouldn't fret too much if I were you,' Alain said, laughing, 'for there will always be wars when this one is over.'

Even Jacques smiled at that. Alain could coax smiles out of people sunk in gloom. It was part of the sunshine of his nature. There are people born like that, who manage, whatever the particular circumstances of their lives, to shed sunshine over those they meet. I have grown to think over the years that such a gift is beyond price, worth more than the ability to make money or to rise in the world.

When the summer drew to its close Alain started for Cahors again. He would return in the spring when my brother was to be wed.

'You have no thought of making it a double wedding, I suppose?' There was a certain wistfulness in his tone as he put the question.

'Let us wait and see what the next year brings,' I said.

My reasoning was that we were still very young, that there was plenty of time before we settled. There was good sense in my thinking but it was worldly sense and had nothing to do with loving. Had Alain forced me to choose, saying 'Marry me in the spring or I will not bring my flock this way again,' I would have married him at once, but he left me space to choose my own time, and now when I look back down the long tunnel of the years I see that he was wrong. Sometimes a female needs a little forcing.

I had been a year at La Neige and the great hall had shrunk to fit me. My duties were light enough for there was no hard manual work to do. Though the hours were long and Lady Petronella could be exacting, I knew that I was learning manners and skills above my station. Though I was never talented at playing any instrument I could at least pick out an accurate tune, and I was graceful in the measure and sweet-voiced in the song. My embroidery and lace-making attracted praise and I loved to sit in one of the tiny rooms that led off the spiral stairs with the winter sunlight speckling the stone floor and draw the brilliant silk through the velvet or silk that flowed over my lap. At those times I could dream ahead, building in my mind the timbered inn with its cobbled yard and warm rooms and shining wood where Alain could be mine host and I could sit in a gown embroidered by my own hands and sing for the customers when they requested it.

I was seated thus one day when a footfall on the narrow landing outside the open door made me look up. The man with black hair and cool grey eyes who stood gazing at me had not changed since I had seen him riding with Anne Foix up to his grandmother's castle.

'Sir Benet.' I would have curtsied were it not for the silk billowing about me, but he made a dismissive gesture with his hand and stepped within.

'So you are in service here now?' He regarded me with some amusement. 'I fancied that you might wheedle your way in somehow.'

'I did no such thing,' I said flatly, forgetting my manners and the respect I owed. 'Lady Petronella asked me to come, and since it is always good to better oneself I agreed.'

'You have not lost your sharp tongue,' he observed. 'I like a maid who is not all sugar and spice.'

'Oh, there are both in me, sir,' I said, 'but I save them for my sweetheart.'

'You have only one?' He raised his dark eyebrows.

'As you have only one wife, sir.'

'I have no wife,' he said.

'Oh, I thought the Lady Anne — ' I was flustered.

'My cousin, Anne Foix, proved faithless and rushed into wedlock with a friend of mine,' he said. 'I danced at their reception.'

'I am very sorry,' I said meekly.

'Sorry she jilted me or sorry that you missed my dancing?' He laughed softly, his eyes fixed on my reddening cheeks. 'I am not nursing a broken heart or even my injured pride, I assure you. Anne is a beautiful fool. Anyway it weakens the strain when cousins make a habit of wedding and breeding too often. You should hear my grandmother on the subject.'

'But if you felt affection?' I ventured.

'If I can feel affection for one then I can feel it for another. Tell me about your sweetheart, for there was a certain softness in your voice when you spoke. Is he a fine lord who likes to dabble in the ditch?'

That was insult pure and sharp. I sprang up, the silk sliding unheeded to the stone, and said heatedly,

'He is an honest shepherd, Sir Benet, and I was never in a ditch in my life!'

'What white skin you have,' he said unperturbed. 'White skin and flaming hair and excellent teeth.'

He had stepped close and gripped my chin in his hand. The sapphire ring he wore pressed into my flesh.

'I am not a horse for your inspection,' I said, jerking my head aside.

'No, she is not,' said Lady Petronella beyond the door. 'She is a good girl and in my service, and not for your fumbling, Benet.'

'I was jesting with her,' he said calmly, letting me go and turning to bow to her.

'She is under my protection so let her alone,' she answered. 'What are you doing, riding here alone without any warning?'

'Must I give warning now when I visit my own home?' he countered.

'As La Neige is mine and not entailed then you are here as guest and not owner. Remember that before you piddle-paddle with my maids!'

'You took this one from the village. Why?'

'She amuses me,' Lady Petronella

said. 'You know my theory, that it is only upbringing that separates lord from peasant? Well, she is living proof of it. No other of my well-born attendants can match this one for grace or charm.'

'The grace I'll grant,' he said, laughing. 'The charm I've yet to see.'

'She does not cast her pearls before all. Benet, what are you doing here?'

'I had a fancy to ride and visit you. You are my nearest living relative, after all.'

'Very much living,' she said tartly. 'When I am in danger of dying I will let you know.'

'I may be the first to go,' he told her. 'The war grows hotter. The English surround Calais and swear to remain until every citizen is starved out. His Grace King Philip must bestir himself very soon if he is not to lose his chief port.'

'The king prefers to amuse himself with tournaments,' Lady Petronella said. 'The Valois are living proof of my theory. They have married their cousins for generations, and this makes them as unstable as water and as treacherous. In a Valois Court each must look to himself. You would do well to remember that.'

'Why, Grandmother, you sail close to the shores of treason,' he said softly.

'And how you would love to inform against me! But if you ever did and made someone believe your charge,' she replied, 'remember that the estates of a traitor are forfeit to the crown and the king might not bestow them upon you. It is wiser for you to wait until I die in the normal course of nature and then you are more likely to inherit La Neige.'

'Why who else would you leave it to?' I asked.

'To a peasant perhaps to prove my theory. Zabillet, tonight wear the green gown and leave your hair loose. We shall have dancing to welcome my grandson.'

She patted my cheek and swept out,

Benet in her wake. I stood where I was, the silk crumpled on the floor, her final words revolving in my mind.

The fortress was unentailed. She might will it where she chose. The castle in Lorraine had descended to her son and thence to Benet. Rumour said it was a fine estate, so if she left La Neige elsewhere she would not be leaving him destitute. If she left it to a peasant — ? I told myself that my thoughts were foolishness. She had been baiting her grandson in the way of an old person who seeks to bend younger relatives to their will, but the thoughts remained in me, pressed down, never brought out to be examined in the light of common sense. That evening I wore the green dress and let my hair hang free, curling thickly about my face, the longer strands reaching my hips. I was not yet seventeen and I was — no, not beautiful for my nose was too broad and my mouth too wide — something to look at twice. Benet looked more than twice. He danced with me, his cool eyes on my face, and when I took my turn at singing he twisted about on his stool and watched me closely.

That night when I was preparing for bed Lady Petronella came, tapping first upon the door in the polite way she had.

'I require company tonight and for the next few nights,' she said. 'There is a pallet in my room.'

She often took it into her head to have one of the maidservants sleep near her, but this was the first time she had requested my presence. The thought flashed into my head that Benet slept in a room at the top of the tower and had free access to the smaller rooms opening off the stairs.

The pallet was laid on the floor at the foot of her huge bed. I waited until she had climbed between the coverlets and then lay down. From the high piled pillows where she was ensconced she said,

'When you have children prepare to

be disappointed, Zabillet.'

'My lady, surely that depends on the father,' I made bold to say.

'You are right.' She chuckled slightly. 'My husband was an epicure — do you know what an epicure is, Zabillet?'

'No, my lady.'

'One who loves only the fine and the delicate and the priceless. Benet — my husband Benet after whom my son and grandson were named — was an epicure. He was also a Cathar, but was clever, or cowardly, enough to outwardly conform. Perhaps he was no true Cathar for they despise worldly wealth believing that, like all material things, it is created by the Demiurge, the King of the world whom some call Lucifer. Howbeit he enjoyed his possessions. He enjoyed me. Does that surprise you?'

I said that it didn't. Old as she was I could still discern traces of beauty in her face.

'We had only one son,' she resumed. 'He was gentle and sweet-tempered which is to say he was timid and weak. He fell in love with his cousin and married her a few months after my husband's death. I was still shocked by my own grief and so did nothing to dissuade him. She was a poor creature, soft as thistledown and as ephemeral. She did not survive the birth of her child and not long after that my son died of the coughing sickness. Apart from my Foix cousins Benet is my only relative. He already holds the property in Lorraine and looks to be master here when I am gone. I have reared him as well as I can, and he is a man now who goes his own way, but I worry about him.'

I thought that, at twenty-six, he was too old to be worried over by a grandmother, but as it would have been rude to say so I kept silent.

'Have you and the shepherd troth plighted yourselves?' she asked suddenly.

'Not officially, but we have a private agreement. We will wed in a year or two, my lady.'

'You are wise not to run into matrimony,' she said. 'Too many girls are wed at thirteen and fourteen and worn out with childbearing and hard work by the time they reach their twenties. It is not intelligent of them. You are wise to delay.'

'It is not for lack of loving him,' I said defensively.

'I heard talk of his really being the priest's bastard. Is it true?'

'He bought his legitimacy from the Bishop at Carcassonne.'

'Aye, one can purchase almost anything from a bishop,' she said dryly. 'Well, I'm sure he is a good young man. Handsome too from what I saw. Nice manners.'

'We loved each other the instant we met,' I confided. 'One look joined us. It was like a miracle.'

'Was it so?' Her voice had softened. 'Yes, child, I too have known that moment of recognition, when you look into the eyes of another and see your shared pasts reflected there.'

'And your husband felt the same way?' I said.

'My husband?' Her pretty laugh lightened the gloom of the arched chamber. 'I was not talking about my husband! Go to sleep, Zabillet. I did not request your presence here so that you could keep me awake all night with your chattering.'

She had taken me into her room as a sign to her grandson that I was a respectable maiden despite my origins, I guessed, and I allowed myself a small smile in the dimness because if Benet La Neige ever laid a finger on me he would swiftly learn that I could take care of myself. He stayed for over a month and had little opportunity to do anything other than watch me as I carried out my duties. Often during those days I would look up to see his cold grey gaze fixed on me, with a queer speculative expression in them. Yet when he partnered me in the evenings he danced with the other maidservants too, lingering longer with

Claude and Marie. Miguette had left to marry her betrothed and Laura had decided to enter a convent and would not dance. I knew the other girls thought him handsome. For my own part I admitted to myself that he had a certain elegance but Alain, in the same fine clothes, would have been even more elegant.

I thought of him making his slow journey back to Cahors, being greeted by his mother, telling her how the summer had been and how much he loved me. Did he tell her how much he loved me, and did she feel a tiny dart of jealousy when she thought of the unknown girl who had stolen his affections? I wondered too if she would ever tell him about Father Hubert and how she had felt when she found herself with child by a priest. Father Hubert would have been a young man then. It was hard to imagine him as anything other than gnarled and lined.

That was a warmer winter than most, with the snow remaining a shorter time, and the first flowers thrusting their heads through the greening earth some weeks before their time. It was weather for walking and I sometimes slipped away and walked on the rough ground behind the fortress, hoping but not expecting to see Alain approaching with his flocks.

What I did see was Benet La Neige riding away from the building with his squire and a couple of grooms in attendance. He was dressed in a furred cloak for a long journey and his saddle-bags weighed down the attendant mules. When he saw me he spurred over the half-frozen ground towards me.

'So there you are, Mistress, hiding away when your companions came to bid me farewell. Or are you secretly grieving because I am returning to Lorraine?'

'I didn't know that you were going anywhere,' I said honestly.

'Then you dream your way through the conversations that go on around you,' he said. 'I am going back to Lorraine to oversee the estate, and then I will join His Grace in Paris. With winter gone the campaign will doubtless resume with renewed ferocity. Are you not fearful that I may be wounded or killed?'

'Your grandmother would grieve,' I evaded.

'Oh, she would quickly recover her spirits.' His mouth was bitter. 'I have never lived up to her expectations of me. My father never lived up to them either.'

'You remember him?' I looked up at him as he sat his mount, recalling that day when I had first seen him riding down into the valley with the peregrine falcon on his glove.

'As well as I remember the first time I saw a redheaded brat playing in the meadow by her grandam's domus,' he said, so exactly matching my drift of thought that I felt a chill as if someone had just stepped over my grave.

'I was very rude,' I said meekly.

'In that you have not altered, but you amuse my grandmother. I only succeed in irritating her, so it's best I go to irritate the English instead. Do you wish me God speed, Zabillet?'

'Yes, sir, with a good will,' I said. 'Please come back safe.'

'Oh, I will, Mistress Zabillet. You may depend on it,' he said coolly. 'Be a good serving maid until I come back.'

He leaned, drew the tip of his whip down the side of my face, and rode off, calling to his attendants to follow him, leaving me in the half-frozen ground, the shiver that convulsed me having nothing to do with the weather.

The spring came fully before February was out and with it came Alain, and my heart gambolled like one of the new lambs born at Christ-tide. Oh, but Alain for all that his tunic and leggings were homespun and his hands calloused was worth all the La Neiges with their fine garments and splendid horses.

'You are the loveliest thing in the whole of France,' he whispered, holding me tightly. 'I drove my mother crazy with talking about you during the winter. We must be wed next spring come what may, my loveling. Promise me.'

In the following spring I would be nearly eighteen, past the age when most local girls were wed. It would be sheer cruelty to deny the consummation again.

'Next spring,' I told him, winding my arms about his neck. 'By next spring I will be fit to play hostess in your tavern.'

'I am more interested in the wife in my bed,' he said, laughing. 'Will you be troth plighted before witnesses now?'

'Where is the point? I am not going to run away or change my mind before next spring,' I said.

'Are you truly mine, Zabillet?' He held me away and looked searchingly into my face. 'Since you entered the service of Lady Petronella I have sometimes wondered — it seems you grow a little further off each time I come.'

'Only that I may be even closer when we are wed,' I told him.

In that summer my brother Reynaud wed his Denise. She was a pretty, vapid girl, somewhat spoiled by her widowed mother, but well enough in her way. Certainly Reynaud considered her the most beautiful girl ever born. 'Though he could pick up six like her by walking up the street,' I told Israel when I went to see him one day shortly before the wedding. He had not attended since though he was willing enough to enter the priest's house he drew the line at the church lest it give his friend a false hope of converting him.

'He does not think so,' Israel said. 'Be glad of it. Love only flourishes when we believe our lover to be entirely unique. Reynaud will be a contented husband and she will make a good mother for his children. Where is Alain today?'

'He went fishing with Father Hubert,' I told him.

'It is good that they are friends,' Israel said. 'And you? You still hold the young man off, promising next year, sometime, maybe?'

'Next year for sure,' I said. 'It will be the better for the keeping.'

'Unlike the fish,' Israel said and chuckled, but his next remark startled me. 'Why do you fear marriage?' he asked.

'Fear it? I long for it,' I said decidedly.

'Yet from season to season you delay,' he said.

'Because I don't want to be poor,' I told him. 'The girls who wed too young grow old too fast. I want something better and so does Alain.'

'You could well afford to wed now,' he said, gently unrelenting. 'You have your grandmother's domus and your nest-egg — no, I've spoken of it to

196

nobody so you need not frown — and Alain has profits from his flocks and will own another house and vineyard in the fullness of time. Do you want to be the richest woman in the world?'

'No, only in France,' I said, and laughed. 'No, that is but jesting. I want a tavern where Alain can be mine host, a respected citizen and member of a Guild instead of a shepherd who is absent from home half the year. I want him to wear a fine tunic and a cloak edged with fur and ride a horse instead of going everywhere on his feet.'

'And a fine gown or two for yourself I dare say?' he said.

'I like to look well. There's no harm in that.'

'No harm at all,' he agreed amiably. 'I am probably in error but I have lived long enough to fear delay. If you crave wine and water is at hand drink the water lest you never get a chance to slake your thirst. But I am only a cautious old man who rambles on without much purpose. Here comes better company for you.'

The better company was Alain, carrying a creel of silvery fish, his rod over his shoulder while Father Hubert trailed behind with his cassock hitched up and a beam on his brown face.

'It's a pity it is not Lent,' he called, 'for the fish are fairly leaping out of the water. You look so cool and fresh, Zabillet. You must share your secret with us for we are sweating like horses ridden too hard.'

'It is healthy to sweat,' Alain said, putting down the creel, and throwing himself full length on the grass. 'Zabillet is the exception to the rule. She has a skin like the petals of a lily without any effort at all.'

'Save that I never sit out for long in the sun,' I said, rising from the step and drawing my veil over my head. 'If Lady Petronella were to see me now she would scold me heartily.'

'We conduct our lives so as not to annoy the Lady Petronella,' Alain said.

'She has been good to me,' I said, a

trifle sharply for the dryness in his tone irritated me. 'I can never be sufficiently grateful.'

'I meant no disrespect, sweetheart,' he said, reaching up to tug playfully at my skirt.

'There is something happening down in the village,' Israel broke in, looking away down the path. Alain stood up again at that and we all looked at the cluster of coloured ants swarming along the cobbles. From where we stood I could have cupped street and houses in my two palms.

'Something has happened,' Alain said, and took my hand, hurrying me down the path.

'Don't leave the fish to stink in the sun!' Father Hubert cried over his shoulder to Israel as he followed.

In the street the ants resolved themselves into neighbours, all talking at once.

'What is going on?' I ran to where my parents stood. It was my father who answered.

'Some soldiers brought word to La Neige that Calais is taken.'

'They surrendered?' My brother Jacques had joined the group. 'It's not possible!'

'After a year under siege they had not even rats to eat,' Simon said. 'They were starving.'

'Better they all starved,' my brother said fiercely, 'than surrender.'

'You've had a full belly all your life,' my father said, 'so 'tis easy for you to talk.'

'Do you grudge the feeding of me?' Jacques demanded. 'It's not my choice to stay here and live on your bounty.'

'Watch your mouth,' my father said without heat and caught him a blow that sent him reeling.

'Let us not quarrel,' Father Hubert said, having caught us up. 'In times of disaster we ought to be united. Where are the soldiers now?'

'They went back to the fortress for a meal,' my father said, scowling at Jacques. 'What they say bears the stamp of truth. They said that the six chief burghers of the city came out with halters around their necks and offered themselves for hanging if Edward of England would only spare the other citizens.'

'He did not — ?' Father Hubert looked apprehensive.

'He was going to,' Guillemotte chipped in, 'but good Queen Philippa went on her knees and begged him to spare them. So he spared them but so many in the city died already of hunger that it made little mark. We have lost our chief port, Father, for the English will hang on to it for a thousand years and steal all the wool trade.'

'Will you lose profit?' I said anxiously to Alain.

'I don't know, love.' He spoke absently, his mind evidently on something else.

'What is it, Alain?' I tugged impatiently on his sleeve.

'The Prince of Wales — was he

with his father?' he asked of nobody in particular.

'One of the soldiers said he was,' Jean said.

'He is Lord of Aquitaine,' Alain said uneasily. 'He may turn south and march his troops to his domain. My mother is alone at Cahors.'

'If it is the prince's own domain he'll not be invading,' Father Hubert reminded him.

'His men make small account of that when they come through Cahors,' Alain said.

'You are going back before the autumn comes?' I looked at him in dismay.

'I think I must.' He took my hand again and drew me aside. 'Zabillet, if I gather my sheep and leave now I can sell them along the Aragon border and be with my mother before the prince reaches Gascony. It is a duty I owe her, for she has nobody now except me.'

'Oh, I don't want you to leave yet,' I said, and felt tears well in my eyes.

'Then come with me,' he said. 'Zabillet, Father Hubert would marry us now and then we can travel together. You are always saying you want to leave Fromage.'

'But not behind a flock of sheep!' I cried, and bit my lip, seeing the hurt on his face. 'Alain, I want a big wedding with the whole village here to dance and sing and ourselves leaving on horseback with our saddlebags stuffed.'

'You will not alter your mind?'

I almost did, there and then, for his dark eyes were full of pain and his hand on mine was tender, but I shook my head.

'Gather your sheep and go into Aragon,' I said. 'When spring comes you will return and I will marry you. Go south and hurry back in spring.'

'Will you help me round up my sheep?' I heard him say through the chattering of the crowd. I shook my head.

'Lady Petronella expects me back

before this hour,' I said. 'Alain, I promise you — '

'In spring then,' he said, and heedless of the people kissed me long and deep and went away towards the valley where his sheep grazed, without a backward look. I let him go, myself turning upwards towards La Neige, and thought how sad it was that two who loved so well should be always going in opposite directions.

8

The autumn seemed so long and dull now that Alain had left. There was more rain than was customary at that season and the villagers had to rush to get in the crops before they were sodden. I realise as I speak that I refer to 'the villagers' as if they were separate and apart from me. The truth, I suppose, is that I was steadily moving away from them, my life lived at La Neige making me a stranger. I tried to tell myself it was not so, but I knew that it was when my mother laid a clean white cloth over the table in our domus when I ate with the family after Mass. The cloth was used only for guests.

Autumn became winter at last and the sight of the first snow was a relief if only because it denoted the passing of time. At La Neige we sat at our looms and tapestry frames while Lady Petronella read to us from one of her books. She owned six very beautifully bound manuscripts including the romantic tale of Charlemagne and Roland over which we all sighed, and another on Court etiquette which we were supposed to pay particular attention to, though it was unlikely that any of us would ever get near enough to a royal Court to put its precepts into practice.

It was in the month of February that rumour reached us of a mysterious and terrible sickness that was spreading from the southern ports. There were always summer epidemics, as there are now, but this was different. This was an illness that killed within hours, and the symptoms were dreadful. Huge boils erupted in groin and armpit; the skin turned black; the victim smelt putrid even before dissolution. The disease also took another form, with no boils or stink, but simply suffocation as the poison turned inward. I speak now of what we knew later. When it first started it was only vague rumour carried by pedlars and by men returning from the wars.

'They say the disease began in the Orient,' Father Hubert said in his Sunday sermon. 'It was suspected that this might be a punishment inflicted by God upon the infidels there, but now people in Italy and even Marseille are dying of it, good Christians falling like raindrops and nobody can tell why. For ourselves we shall continue to pray for the scourge to pass us by. But who can gainsay the Will of God?'

We discussed it afterwards, he and Israel and myself, sitting round the table in the priest's domus. It was too cold to sit outside as we liked to do, but the fire smoked badly and we had perforce to leave the door open.

'The Will of God?' Israel spoke thoughtfully, then shook his head.

'The Lord does chastise His children,' Father Hubert said.

'Sometimes I think we blame the

Lord for much we bring upon ourselves,' Israel said.

'Through sin,' Father Hubert said gloomily.

'Or stupidity,' Israel amended.

'Plagues that begin in the cooler months are rare,' Father Hubert mused. 'I have noticed that in damp and heat illness is more prevalent. Yet this began during the autumn and now is afflicting many communities. We must pray.'

'And wash,' said Israel.

'You cannot wash away sin,' Father Hubert said. 'Pontius Pilate tried.'

'I was not thinking of sin,' Israel said. 'I was thinking of the Greek goddess, Hygienia.'

'A pagan idol?' Father Hubert looked unhappy.

'Hygienia was goddess of cleanliness,' Israel said. 'You must know that many of these gods and goddesses were merely personifications of particular virtues and qualities. In Ancient Greece plagues were more efficiently controlled than in our own time. It might not hurt to take a lesson from the past.'

'I have noticed too that during times of plague the death rate among Jews is much lower than in the rest of the community.'

'I believe that our habit of regular bathing is the reason for that,' Israel said. 'Even you will not say it is because we commit fewer sins than our Christian brethren.'

'Too frequent washing can weaken the frame,' Father Hubert said.

'Then you will not take my advice?' Israel glanced at him.

'Which is?'

'Order your parishioners to wash their clothes in hot water and scrub out their dwellings. Then they must wash themselves all over every day. If they find it difficult to do that let them go up to the spring and sluice themselves in the running water. And once a week is not often enough for delousing. It should be done twice a week. I believe that will help to keep down the mortality rate if the plague comes here.'

'It makes sense, Father,' I urged, ranging myself firmly on Israel's side. 'Anything is worth the trying.'

Father Hubert bit his lip and then nodded.

'Go and ring the bell, Zabillet,' he instructed. 'Israel, since this is your idea you may put it forward.'

'Then you must assemble your people outside the church,' Israel said.

'Stubborn!' Father Hubert muttered, rising.

I went to tug upon the bell-rope that clanged only for births and deaths and emergencies. Father Hubert had rung the Angelus regularly in his younger days, but now he had let the custom lapse.

The sound of the bell brought everybody hurrying back, faces alert and sharp with worry.

'What's to do? Are the English coming?' Guillemotte demanded breathlessly. 'Girl, stop tugging at that rope. We all heard you. Father, what's wrong?'

'Israel has an idea,' Father Hubert said.

There was an instant's silence. Then Guillemotte cried, 'You've had the bell rung and brought us all back up the hill because the Jew had an idea? Have you gone stark staring crazy, Father?'

'Only listen to what he has to say and then you will see,' Father Hubert said.

Israel, finding two hundred pairs of eyes fixed on him, quailed and rallied, rapidly setting out his plan.

'But it's not the season for washing,' my mother said in bewilderment. 'We take a bath every summer. In this cold we will freeze.'

'Not if you fill wooden tubs with hot water and salt,' Israel told her.

'He's trying to turn us all into Jews,' Jeanne said shrilly. 'He wants to wash off our Christianity.'

'That is nonsense,' Father Hubert said briskly. 'It is a way of avoiding this new sickness, that's all.'

'But it won't come to Fromage

anyway,' Simon said confidently.

'How do you know that?' my father enquired.

'Everybody knows that the Jews — the other Jews, Israel — poison wells and so bring sickness. Now we all know that Israel would never do any such thing.'

'How do you know anyone else does it?' Father Hubert demanded. 'Who told you?'

'I don't need telling,' Simon retorted. 'It's common knowledge.'

'Not all common knowledge is accurate,' Israel said peacefully.

'Surely sickness is God's punishment for sin,' the Widow Foret piped up. 'It's God's Will.'

'If that's true then we will get the sickness whether we wash or no,' Father Hubert said, 'unless you think we can alter God's Will by soaking in a hot tub.'

'Will you be taking a bath yourself, Father?' Gilles asked suspiciously.

'I shall be first into the hot water,'

Father Hubert assured him, 'and, old as I am, I'll knock down any idiot who says that thereby I have washed off my Christianity.'

'What about the ones up at the castle?' Guillemotte asked. 'Will they be taking baths?'

'We already do, four times a year,' I said smugly, 'and wash our hands and faces every day.'

'We shall do it then?' Father Hubert looked from face to face.

I don't know what decision would have been made had there not been a sudden commotion down at the bottom of the hill. A horse was whinnying in fright, ears flat against his head, his forelegs kicking frantically as he sought to dislodge a burden on his back.

'Stand back,' Israel said, as much authority in his voice as any priest's, and went down the track to the plunging, snorting beast.

'Be careful, my friend. The horse will trample you!' Father Hubert cried.

Everybody was streaming down the

hill towards the horse whose dangling rein Israel had now caught, and as we watched, he blew up the nostrils of the terrified animal. The rolling eyes ceased to reveal their whites and the horse stood tremblingly.

'A trick I learned from a Moslem once,' Israel said modestly. 'Now let us see what we have that causes this beast such fear — no, stand back and cover your mouths and noses!'

The command was superfluous.

'Dear God, the stench!' My mother turned aside to vomit into the grass.

'A merchant from the clothes,' Israel said. 'On his way from the south, poor soul. Father Hubert, get sacking and ropes. He must be buried.'

'It's a fine horse,' my brother said.

'The horse must be slaughtered and the carcass buried deep,' Israel said. 'As a precaution.'

I had caught only a glimpse of the blackened, pistuled countenance and my gorge rose as I hastily turned away.

'Are we to take baths or not?' Israel said to nobody in particular.

'Margot, come and help me boil water,' Guillemotte ordered. 'The rest of you back off until your garments have been cleansed. Move yourselves! You heard what good Master Israel said.'

I touched my mother briefly on the arm, and for an instant she flinched as if I carried the death myself. It would grow worse with people fearing to meet together lest one infect the others or, God seeing a crowd, kill many at one stroke.

That was the beginning of the Great Death, and you who never lived through it cannot begin to comprehend.

They say a third of the world died, whole villages wiped out until nobody was left alive to do the burying, and the blackened, stinking corpses lay above ground, torn by wolves and pecked by birds while their deserted homes gradually fell into disrepair,

215

roofs sagging, walls cracking, vegetable plots running wild. The disease made no distinction between high and low; the lord perished with his servant, the maid with her mistress. In Avignon half the population died, in Carcassonne every Franciscan perished and all but seven Dominicans.

At Fromage we were guided by Israel and Father Hubert who, together, comprised a formidable partnership. Every day tubs of water, drawn from the river and salted, were heated for the baths; every week the houses were scrubbed and scoured and the vermin killed; twice a week there were delousing sessions and the washing of linen. There were tree trunks felled to block the southern road that nobody might carry infection from the south. Israel was of the opinion that the disease could be carried on the person and breathed in by others, and though most thought his opinion grotesque it had to be admitted that in Fromage people stayed healthy. At the castle Lady Petronella put Israel's theories in to practice too, any visitor having to submit to a hot bath and a delousing before he was allowed within the precincts. But there were few travellers since it was still winter and many of the roads were flooded. What news filtered through to us was all of death and dying.

In the midst of it all Benet La Neige returned, coldly elegant, submitting with an ill grace to the hot bath and delousing his grandmother insisted upon before she would admit him.

'Though why you should think it makes any difference,' he said, sitting later with a mug of wine in the hall, 'I cannot think.'

'I have the evidence of my own senses,' Lady Petronella said tartly. 'Since the merchant was buried nobody has died here or down in the village. Is it thus elsewhere?'

He shook his head, his face darkening. 'Even in royal households,' he said, 'the pestilence creeps. It has killed Alfonzo of Castile, did you know that? At my own estate in Lorraine we have already lost twenty of our labourers. They are blaming the Jews, hunting them down with dogs, burning them in their houses.'

'In Fromage we have more sense,' his grandmother said. 'The Pope ought to put a stop to it.'

'Has your priest not heard? His Holiness has issued an edict designed to protect Jews but few listen or obey,' he said.

'You rode alone all the way from Lorraine?' She raised her eyebrows.

'It is safer so. Oh, I did fall in with one along the way. I had almost forgot. A pedlar on the road from Cahors. We shared a cup of wine together and compared death rates. He had a letter about him.'

It could only be for me. I was seated with the other girls but I forgot my manners and rose, my face flushing with eagerness as I cried,

'Oh, it must surely be for me!'

'Aye, the name upon it is Zabillet d'Aude.' He drew the thin, sealed paper from his pouch and gave me a mocking look. 'I did not know that your rustic sweetheart could read.'

'He cannot, but someone will have written to his dictating. May I have it?' I held out my hand.

'But if you cannot read it either,' he said teasingly, holding it just out of reach, 'what's the use?'

'Cease tormenting the child,' Lady Petronella said. 'Give it to me, Benet. Shall I read it for you, Zabillet?'

I hesitated, unwilling to have Alain's message read out in the presence of everybody.

'Come to my room after supper,' Lady Petronella said kindly. 'I shall read it for you when we are alone.'

I would have given much to hear it then, but she put it away and continued to question Benet about affairs in Lorraine.

The war with England had dwindled because of the pestilence, with English soldiers fleeing back across the Channel though there were already reports that there was death in England too. Blown by the wind or carried upon the breath it was said, and the ports lay idle, ships filled with rotting goods and dead and dying men. Preachers wandering through every land warned that the end of the world was approaching and called upon men everywhere to repent.

'God have mercy on us all,' Lady Petronella said. 'Let's to supper while we can still enjoy our food.'

Supper seemed such a long-drawn-out meal that evening. I could scarce swallow for thinking of the letter. I had never received a letter in my life nor written one — dictated, I should say. You are so fortunate, Sister, to have been so highly educated, though I have noticed that in those who can read the memory is less acute. So, though I am sixty-three years old, my mind is still sharp and pictures of the past rise like foam on its surface. That great hall with the Lady Petronella cutting her meat neatly with the point of her knife and her keen old eyes fixed upon the pale oval of her grandson's face as he ate and talked and quaffed the wine in the cup at his elbow. Myself, seated on the bench with the other serving maids, my thick hair netted, my face betraying impatience as course succeeded course and the fire sank into ashes.

At last she pushed her plate away and rose.

'Attend upon me after the dishes have been removed,' she said, and moved in her stately fashion towards the stairs.

Benet had also risen, a chicken wing still in his hand, bowing politely. His grandmother was, I believe, the only woman in the world he respected. He had been occupied in talk of the pestilence during supper but now his cold grey eyes moved towards me.

'You have grown meeker,' he observed. 'Seated like a little mouse among the

221

others. Have you nothing to say to me?'

'Welcome home, Sir Benet,' I said, one eye on the servants who were clearing the dishes.

'Is she always so demure?' he demanded of the others.

There were giggles at his deigning to notice them. That irritated me, for my companions were accomplished and intelligent young women, so why must they blush and bridle simply because a gentleman was present?

'Please excuse me,' I said formally. 'I must attend my lady.' And have my letter read to me. I fairly flew up the stairs into the bedchamber beyond the upper gallery where a fire burned merrily in a brazier and Lady Petronella sat with the letter open in her hands and her fine-boned old face illuminated like a manuscript by the glow of the flames.

'The dishes are cleared, my lady,' I said breathlessly.

'Child, I would have that task to be

unending,' she said, her tone so heavy that the smile on my lips faltered and failed.

'The letter is — it is meant for me?' I sat down on a stool without waiting for permission.

She bowed her head, her long fingers almost transparent in the firelight. 'From Alain Berger?' I said.

'From his mother, written by a clerk from Cahors.'

'His mother? But why should his mother write to me?' I said, made stupid by the fear that gripped me.

'Mistress Zabillet — ' She drew a long breath, then said with brutal simplicity, 'He is dead, child. Of the pestilence two months since. His mother sends word to his sweetheart. She writes — '

'I don't want to hear it,' I said. 'I don't want to hear it.'

'It is your letter. You have a right to hear what she says.'

'And a right not to hear. If he is — is dead what use the hearing the news all over again?' I heard myself say.

My voice sounded small and cold. I was aware that my whole body was cold despite the heat from the brazier. I was numb to my fingertips with the ice that encased me.

'She says that he died very quickly,' Lady Petronella told me.

'That's good,' I said foolishly. 'That's very good.'

'He was a pleasant lad.' She sighed and looked down at the letter. 'This might carry infection, if what the Jew believes is true.'

'So burn it,' I said. 'Burn it.'

'You don't wish me to put it in a safe place for you until the pestilence is past?'

I shook my head slowly from side to side, feeling a great heaviness descend upon me.

She held the paper a moment longer and then fed it into the flames where it blazed briefly and then fell into black ash. Brief as Alain's life, I thought.

'My dear, I am so very sorry,' she

said gently, more gently than I had ever heard her speak.

'May I be excused?' I said, and part of me stood aside from myself, thinking, 'How politely and softly Zabillet speaks, not forgetting her training in manners even at this moment of grief.' It was not grief, of course. Grief would come later, much later when the knowledge had sunk into my consciousness, ripping my core into a thousand pieces. At that instant there was only the ice enclosing my heart holding me together.

'Yes, of course,' she said, and I made my curtsey and left the gallery, groping my way down the spiral stairs as if I had been struck blind. In the hall beyond the screens someone struck a rippling chord upon a lute. A happy tune to hear in the midst of death. I wrenched open the heavy door and stepped out into the inner courtyard, hearing someone behind me exclaim at the sudden draught.

The melting snow wept from the cornices, and the wind piled the remaining drifts into the corners. The cobbles were rimed with slush and the soles of my shoes slithered as I went towards the drawbridge. Outside the castle the landscape was unfamiliar in the moonlight. The folds and wrinkles of the ground were black shadows that crossed and recrossed the pale crags. The village below lay in darkness, as did the church and the priest's house. Only the stars silvered the sky as the moon moved, slow and majestic, behind a bank of cloud.

Alain would not be coming in the spring. It was early spring already though the weather tried to deny it. In a week or two I would have spent time looking over the hills for the first sight of his flock. No need to do that now, slipping away from my loom or tapestry frame to scan the horizon.

I looked down into the moat on which thin fragments of ice floated like corpses. The world was coming to an end and with sudden clarity I knew that I cared little if everybody on the face of the earth vanished as long as Alain was spared.

'You are not thinking of jumping in, I hope?' Benet La Neige said at my shoulder.

I turned, bracing myself against the parapet.

'My grandmother has just informed me that your sweetheart is dead,' he said. 'I am truly sorry, Mistress.'

'Why?' I said bluntly. 'You didn't know him. He was only a shepherd, you know. Of little account among the nobility.'

'I am sorry for it because you loved him and his death will bring you pain,' Benet said. 'I know that I have often jested and mocked with you, but I meant no hurt. I would not have you hurt, Zabillet.'

'Thank you, sir.' I opened my mouth to say more — I don't know what it would have been — and the ice that encased me cracked wide open and plunged me into sobbing. I have never been a woman who wept easily and I did not weep easily now, for the tears were scalding and my cries were moans of anguish. I felt that I knew what it was like to be cleft in two by a broadsword, hacked to pieces with axes, flung into boiling oil. The physical pain of loss was worse than anything I had ever experienced. I could only think confusedly that it would be a relief to die.

'I will take you to your bed,' he said, and bent suddenly, swinging me up into his arms, carrying me back across the courtyard and up the winding stairs. He laid me upon his own pallet and covered me with his cloak, and sat, holding my hand in both his own as the lamps flickered lower and my cries became moans that shuddered through me. And so, at last, as the stars went out like little lives all over the world, I slept.

9

Lady Petronella took it upon herself to have the villagers informed of Alain's death. I was grateful for that kindness; I could not have endured breaking the news. For days I kept my bed, waking only to weep, caring nothing that Benet came and went with spiced wine and pastries, that the other girls sat with me trying to comfort me. I wanted to be dead, to be struck down by the pestilence, to be past the pain of loss.

Then Lady Petronella herself came, bending her head beneath the lintel, her sharp eyes raking me as she said briskly,

'So you have turned Cathar after all and have embarked on the endura.'

'I am sick,' I said.

'Nonsense, child, you are hoping that you will get sick and so avoid grief,' she said. 'You may succeed if you try hard enough but your body will fight you every step of the way. Have you so little courage? Then you are not the girl I took you to be.'

'I have courage,' I said, stung into sitting up.

'Then use it,' said Lady Petronella, 'and remember you are not the only one who grieves for him. I have already sent a message of condolence to Cahors. But Father Hubert has found and lost a son; he has not taken to his bed in weeping and wailing.'

She was right, of course, and at bottom I was relieved to be scolded into action.

I rose and washed my face and combed the tangles out of my hair and went down to take my place at the table. I swear that I didn't feel like eating one bite but my hunger betrayed me and I ate heartily, enjoying every mouthful.

'You look better, Zabillet,' Benet said from his place at supper. 'We have fretted about you.'

'Because I am eating does not mean my spirits are high, sir,' I said.

'You must give Nature time for healing,' he said, still kindly, and sent down a baked pear from his own plate for me to nibble on.

The next day I walked down into the village, being stopped at intervals by neighbours who came to press my hands and murmur sympathy. When I reached my mother's domus she ran out to embrace me, holding me so lovingly that I began to cry all over again.

'Poor Zabillet, poor little maid!' were her first words. 'We had word of Alain's death. I wanted to come up to La Neige to comfort you, but Jean said that it might not be fitting. He was a good lad, such a good lad. I fear many such are dying.'

'But not here in Fromage? There have been no deaths from the pestilence here?'

'None, thank God. It is a miracle,' she said. 'Zabillet, I believe that good old Jew has some special charm to keep plague from his friends. Your father won't have it so, but these infidels do have certain powers that are kept from Christians.'

'It is a pity his power did not extend to Cahors then,' I said bitterly.

'Poor lad,' my mother said, sighing again. 'Father Hubert has offered Masses for his soul, but in my opinion that boy went straight to heaven. He and you — ?' She paused, looking at me. I shook my head.

'In one way it is a shame,' she said, 'for you might have had a child to comfort you, but in another way — you are still virgin and a ripe prize with your grandmother's domus and the land.'

'I will never marry,' I said sharply.

'Never is a very long time, dear,' my mother said, 'but I am sure you will never cease to love Alain.'

I knew she was right even though I shook my head. I was nearly eighteen, of full age for marriage and the bearing of children. I had no religious vocation. Sooner or later I must wed or live despised.

'I am going to see Father Hubert,' I said. 'I will speak with you again after church on Sunday.'

She nodded, embracing me again, and I went on up to the church. Father Hubert looked as he had looked ever since I could remember, and only a close inspection betrayed a certain tremulousness in his manner, a sadness in his voice.

'Are you better, Zabillet? Lady Petronella said you were quite crushed with grief. It is not right for us to mourn so deeply for our fellow mortals but I fear that we do.'

'It was the Will of God,' I said, not believing it.

'So I tell myself. If he had not hurried back to Cahors then — ah well, as you say, it is God's Will. Now tell us how all goes at La Neige. We heard that Sir Benet was at home again.'

'He stays close out of fear of the pestilence, I think,' I said.

'Who can blame him?' Father Hubert said. 'Thank God all have been spared here so far. From the little I have heard 'tis not so in other places. They say that people are abandoning their own children when they fall sick. Only the good Sisters are tending the dying and then dying themselves. There are few strong enough to sow the corn so when harvest comes — ' He broke off and we sat together in silence.

'I have to go now, Father,' I said. 'I have duties at the castle.'

'Yes, of course.' He blessed me absently, his face sombre. As I turned to go he said abruptly, 'Child don't turn away from life because of Alain's death. You are young and comely and if a good man offers for you take him and be thankful.'

I mumbled some reassurance and escaped, going rapidly down the hill into the valley where my grandmother's domus stood. I think I hoped to find some scrap of cloth, some stick, some memory of Alain, but the domus held only the winter dirt and a sad bird's nest abandoned under the eaves.

'Zabillet, hey!' My brother's voice halted me as he ran to catch me up.

'You are well, Jacques? — but I can see that you are,' I said.

He looked as strong and brown as if the sun had shone all winter through.

'I'm well enough,' he said, the familiar expression of sullen discontent settling over his face. 'I was sorry to hear about Alain. That was a sad blow for you.'

'Yes, it was,' I said shortly, not wanting to dwell on the subject. 'What of you, Jacques? Since the pestilence came the war ceases to rage.'

'The pestilence must end some time,' he said, 'and then men will take up arms again, and I long to be with them. I hunger for it, Zabillet.'

'Father will not help you?' I answered my own question. 'No, of course he will not. He wants your labour on the

235

land especially now that Reynaud has the Foret plot for his own.'

'He is a free man yet makes a serf of his son,' Jacques said. 'If I had but the money for a sword and a horse — I could be free, Zabillet.'

The bag of coins that Lady Petronella had given me was hidden within the domus. It had been for my dowry. Now I wasn't going to be married. I could give it to my brother, hand him his freedom. The impulse to do so was very strong. Yet if I were the means of letting him leave, and he was killed or caught the pestilence in some other town, then the blood guilt would be on my head. And I might need that money myself. If I had given him that money so many lives would have been changed. So many lives, Sister. We take or refuse to take a tiny action and we set in motion forces of which we can only dream.

'I am sorry, Jacques,' I said. 'I wish that I could help you.'

'I shall find a way,' he muttered,

'and when I do Fromage'll not hold me.'

'I hope that you do,' I said sincerely enough, and we walked together back into the village, where we parted. Almost at the top of the hill I met Israel coming down, and he like Father Hubert seemed older and more tremulous.

'You keep well?' He gave me a searching look, then nodded. 'Yes, I see only the traces of tears. You must not neglect to wash yourself because of this sad event. You may feel now there is no virtue in going on, but we must all go on.'

'To what?' I said. 'Do you know, Israel?'

'No, child.' He shook his head gently at me. 'I only count each day, good or bad, as a gift. It is all anyone can do. Give my respects to the demoiselle.'

I promised and went on up to La Neige, pausing at the gate to look up at the high stone and to smile despite my unhappiness.

'What amuses you?' Benet enquired, riding to greet me.

'I was just remembering how nervous I felt when I first came here to serve your grandmother,' I told him.

'You nervous? I'll not believe it,' he exclaimed. 'Why, the first time I laid eyes on you I beheld a piece of red-headed impudence.'

'I hope I am more polite now,' I said.

'And more beautiful. My grandam trained you well.'

I was silent, thinking of the tavern that Alain and I had planned. Oh, but it would have been a success had he only lived!

'Crying again?' He leaned from the saddle and touched my cheek with his gloved forefinger.

'Is there something shameful in grief?' I demanded.

'Yes, but the shame is upon those who would not offer solace,' he said. 'What will you do now, Zabillet? Will you wait upon my grandmother until she is senile and yourself middle-aged, or will you take a rustic as husband and waste your accomplishments in a domus?'

'I would like to leave Fromage,' I said. 'There are other places.'

'For an unprotected maiden? Zabillet, your life and your honour would be at risk.'

'I will learn to look after myself,' I said.

'Why not allow me to do it?' he said.

I stared at him in astonished contempt. He had seemed truly kind and concerned and yet now he sought to impose himself upon me as if I had been born a serf.

'If you want to exercise the *droit de seigneur* then you must look elsewhere,' I said, and turned away.

'Zabillet, you mistake me.' He dismounted, catching my arm, swinging me to face him.

'If I scream,' I said through my teeth, 'your grandmother will soon hear the reason why.'

'Zabillet, I am asking you to be my wife,' he said, releasing my arm but still barring my retreat.

'Oh, that is cruel mockery!' I cried. 'You know how I grieve for Alain and yet — '

'I honour your feelings,' he broke in. 'I could almost envy that shepherd lad for dying if my death would bring such grief. But grief cannot last for ever, Zabillet.'

'It will last my life long,' I said.

'So you will lower yourself into a grave before you have stopped breathing? Not you, Zabillet d'Aude! There is too much love of life in you. I can warm my hands at your hair.'

'I don't love you,' I said flatly. 'If you truly mean to offer marriage — '

'Nothing less!'

'Your grandmother would never permit such a match.' I shook my head and hurried on. 'She has been very kind to me, but she'd drive me from her door if she thought that you, a gentleman, wished to wed me. You say that you honour me, so don't spoil everything for me by making it impossible for me to remain here.'

'If my grandmother could be persuaded to agree how would you say then?' he asked.

'I don't love you,' I repeated obstinately.

'Have you not learned yet that love and marriage often have little to do with each other?' he said impatiently. 'People wed for many reasons but seldom for love. Oh, I love you — have no doubt of that, and honour you sufficiently to offer you wedlock. If you do not actively hate me — Zabillet, I would be content with liking. It would be sufficient for me.'

'It would not be fair to you, sir,' I said, trying to speak calmly though his agitation was beginning to affect me. I had never dreamed that he could speak with such vehemence, the pale oval of his face flushing with emotion.

'At least let me speak to my grandmother,' he said. 'God's death,

Mistress, I am no callow lad to be bullied by an old woman. If she turned you out of doors I would still wed you if you agreed to it.'

'It is too soon,' I stammered.

'And if the pestilence spreads to La Neige it may soon be too late,' he said. 'Zabillet, it is feared the world may be coming to an end. Have you not the right to taste of loving before we meet our Maker?'

I shook my head, but something other than grief was rising in me. I was not yet eighteen, and what he said was true. I had never known the reality of physical love, would never know it if I denied my womanhood.

'You do not hate me?' he said, and a kind of wonder filled me that he should speak so humbly. Nobly born as he was he could not deny my effect upon him. Alain had made me feel cherished. Benet La Neige made me feel powerful. For a moment, in the midst of my grief, I saw myself as the demoiselle of La Neige after Lady Petronella's death.

I would like to say that I saw myself remitting taxes, giving to charity, but this is an honest record. I saw myself in velvet and silk, seated at the table and eating spiced duckling with music playing softly in the background.

'I don't hate you, sir,' I said.

'And if my grandmother smiled upon the idea you might consider marriage?'

'She will not smile,' I said decidedly. 'She took me up on a whim of kindness, but she has a proud name which she will never agree to mingle with peasant blood.'

'We shall see.' He kissed the tips of my fingers and mounted up again. I stood aside as he clattered over the drawbridge, my head beginning to whirl as I realised the full import of what had just occurred. If Lady Petronella did the inconceivable and agreed to the match, then I could become Lady Zabillet La Neige. It was a jump upwards that few ever had the chance of making. Certainly I did not love or desire Benet, but he was handsome and tall and rich, and he had been kind to me in my grieving. Also at twenty-seven he must soon take a wife. As I, at eighteen, ought to take a husband. I turned and wandered past the guarding walls of the moat to where the spring gushed forth. This was the spot where I had first seen Alain, recognised him rather as if we had been together in ages past. I didn't need to close my eyes to see his silver-gold hair that was in such piquant contrast to his dark eyes. I felt his mouth on mine, his hands cupping my breasts — the furthest I ever allowed him to go in loveplay — heard his voice with something of a boy's uncertain roughness in it still. I outlined the grace of his frame, imposing it upon the empty air, and then deliberately I erased it, fading him into nothingness, choking back the last of my futile tears.

When the air was empty of him I drank from the spring and went back to the castle, entering just as Lady

Petronella's voice called impatiently down the spiral stairs,

'Zabillet! Zabillet! Where is the girl?'

'Here, my lady.' I hurried forward.

'Come upstairs,' she ordered.

'I am not tidy,' I began but she interrupted.

'Fiddle to that, girl! Up with you!'

I lifted my skirts and hastily wound myself around the ascending spiral of stone. She had retreated to the bedchamber end of the gallery and seated herself in a high-backed chair. Benet, still booted and spurred, stood looking out into the courtyard.

'My feckless grandson tells me that he means to marry you,' she said without greeting. 'If I refuse my leave and turn you out of doors he will marry you anyway. What say you to that?'

'I have told him that I will abide by your decision,' I said.

'Will you indeed?' Her eyebrows arched in amused scorn. 'How good of Mistress d'Aude to acknowledge the authority of her mistress and to accept my right to make decision. So, if I do turn you out of doors, what will you do?'

'I will go,' I said, 'but not before I tell you that your action is unjust, for I never sought to have your grandson notice me as he will tell you if he is honest.'

'He already told me,' she said. 'You are not of his station, girl. Doubtless you thought of that already?'

'Yes, my lady, but in accomplishments which, thanks to you, I have, then I am grown more than a peasant,' I said boldly.

'Only hear the jade!' she marvelled. 'How she answers me back!'

'I don't mean to be disrespectful,' I said. 'I owe you much, my lady, more than I can ever hope to repay.'

'Oh, there is a way.' She nodded her head, her eyes bright. 'Give me a great-grandson, child, who will be master of La Neige one day when we are all dust. Give me that and I'll wink my eye at your low beginnings.'

I had not expected her to agree and a shiver ran through me as Benet turned from the window and held out his hand, saying,

'Come, Zabillet, and receive my kiss. We shall be speedily married. In these times it would be folly to delay.'

I stepped to him and received his kiss upon my cheek and my lips. His mouth on mine was not unpleasant.

'So the bargain is struck,' Lady Petronella said. 'You will be a good wife to Benet.'

It was not a question. She made a flat statement in the same way she might have told me that I had the qualities of a good cook. At least she did not pretend that I was in love with him.

'I shall send word to Father Hubert to prepare for the ceremony,' she said. 'The chapel here has been disused for so long that I think it more fitting that you be married at the village church. We shall have the reception here.'

'All that is not necessary,' I said

quickly, but she held up an imperious hand.

'My dear, I am not ashamed of my grandson's choice of bride,' she said. 'Your relatives and your neighbours shall share in the rejoicing.'

I was not sure that the last word was the correct one, for surely no bride went with less rejoicing towards her nuptials, but there again I might be wrong. Many girls are forced into far worse alliances through the cupidity of parents and guardians and Benet La Neige was a handsome man, obviously besotted with me. I might have fared worse.

I went to see Father Hubert as soon as the news had been conveyed to him, feeling an obscure guilt at the speed of it all.

'For it is not that I have forgotten my love for Alain, Father,' I said. 'I shall always love him but — '

'But no maid whose sweetheart dies should thereafter deny herself matrimony or children,' he completed kindly. 'My friend, Israel and I both agreed that you must wed and indeed you are wedding beyond our expectations. I am astonished that the Lady Petronella agreed to it.'

'Perhaps she knows a good wife when she sees one,' Israel said.

'And you do not dislike Sir Benet?' Father Hubert peered at me anxiously. He had recently acquired a pair of eye glasses and they made him look like an elderly owl.

'No, he has been very kind to me.'

'And it is certainly time that he took a wife,' Israel remarked. 'The first command is to be fruitful and multiply.'

'I shall do my best,' I said, and went away to my mother's domus. She, having heard the news too, was in a state as near panic as I have ever seen her.

'Such an honour — to have my own daughter wed to the liege lord, but how are we to contrive? Marie and I must have new gowns if we are to attend the ceremony and Father Hubert is so strict against allowing pedlars in these days lest they spread the pestilence. And there must be gifts — and all to do within a week. Oh, if Jacques were here — '

'He is not?'

'He set out for Carcassonne yesterday,' she said. 'He had an errand to perform, he said, but I fear he went simply to annoy Jean for he told only me, and your father was certainly very angry since now he must mend the roof himself. Well, that's not to the purpose — what are we to do for gowns?'

'I shall have two gowns sent to you,' I said, feeling rather grand to be able to say that.

'And will you be happy, child?' She looked at me anxiously much as Father Hubert had done, but he had wanted truth. My mother wanted only to be reassured.

'This is a fine match for me,' I said. 'Why, already I can promise you and

Marie new gowns.'

And when Jacques returned from Carcassonne I would give him the money hidden in the domus so that he could buy a horse and a sword and ride to battle. Benet had no need of my dowry.

'And you are happy?' she persisted.

'I intend to be,' I said stoutly. 'Shall I send a gown for Denise too? Reynaud will wish his wife to be well dressed.'

'Oh, but that will be kind of you, dear.' Her face still comely though she was almost forty years old, lit into a smile.

'I have a generous bridegroom,' I told her, 'who will deny me nothing. You must be glad for me.'

'I am glad. I always hoped for much for you,' she assured me.

I kissed her and left, fearing that she might mention Alain. I had locked up my sadness and thrown away the key, and was determined that nobody should open that box.

That evening Benet put upon my

finger a betrothal ring of emerald set in gold.

'It was my mother's ring,' he said. 'My father gave it to me to keep for my own bride. I am fortunate to have found one with green eyes to match the stone.'

It was a beautiful stone. I turned my hand this way and that to admire it, and responded more warmly to Benet's kiss, but when he would have touched me more intimately I held him off, shaking my head. I would not grant before marriage to a man I didn't love what I had denied my true love.

'You will require garments befitting your new station,' Lady Petronella said.

She had chests of clothes, not all in the latest fashion, but all of fine material with edgings of lace and fur and sleeves trimmed with cloth of gold and silver.

'The new hennins are higher than ever,' she said. 'Two feet high some of them, or conversely, two feet wide. And so loaded with ornament that the poor ladies can scarce hold up their heads. And necklines were shockingly low the last time I was in Lorraine.'

I had no wish for the extremes of fashion, but the garments that were now hastily altered to fit me pleased me greatly. I had three new gowns with two pairs of hanging sleeves with each dress, and two shifts, and a hennin which, if not precisely two feet high, was still fashionably tall, its cone surmounted by a floating veil. I had two cauls of net to hide the heavy tresses of red that must not be allowed to hang loose after my wedding, and hose of silk and shoes and a cloak of fur. I would be a finer lady than I had ever dreamed possible, and that was a curious comfort to me which will show you that I was still shallow and immature.

My father had given his formal consent. No father in his senses would have refused such a match for his daughter.

'He tells me that you have as dowry

the domus in the valley that belonged to your grandmother,' Benet told me. 'I have resolved to allow you to keep it as your own.'

I was glad that he said that, for I could not have borne to have him take the dwelling where Alain had lodged or the land where we had sat planning our future.

I would take the money and give it to Jacques, I decided, and give my little sister, Marie, the domus as her own against the day too when she would be wed. That day might not be far off. She was nearly eleven now, and her courses had already begun. Her figure was plumping out and my mother had told me that many of the village lads were eyeing her with pleasure.

I thanked Benet but kept my resolution to myself. He might regret his generosity if I turned round and immediately bestowed his gift upon someone else. As for the money, Lady Petronella had never mentioned it again, presumably thinking that I had given it to my family. My brother, Jacques, would use it to break free of his servitude.

The preparations for the wedding were being hurried on as fast as if I were pregnant.

'No sense in waiting for the pestilence to reach us,' Lady Petronella said, breaking off in the midst of instructions to the three cooks as to the banquet that would follow the Service.

'I think that the pestilence will not touch Fromage, thanks to Israel's advice,' I said. And neglected to realise that there are worse horrors and greater evil even than pestilence.

10

You will think it most unsuitable for my wedding to be rushed through so quickly, but Benet was determined that it should take place with all speed and I never once begged for delay. If I was going to marry Benet La Neige then I had better do it speedily, I reckoned, before I had second thoughts. It was by no means uncommon, I discovered later, for many weddings to be rushed into at this time of the great plague, either because lads and girls wished to enjoy the delight of love before the black boils came or because property still had to be dowered and distributed. My gown was of pale yellow, a colour most suitable for an Easter bride, and my hair was combed loose under a little cap of cloth of gold. When Lady Petronella tilted her mirror so that I could look at myself I saw a dim, romantic figure with pale face and vibrant hair.

'You are very lovely,' Lady Petronella said.

There was a certain satisfaction in her tone as if she had invented me. I reminded myself that she must have recognised something special in me to invite me into her service and now to allow me to wed into her family, but I lowered my eyelids in the modest way I had been taught and curtseyed.

'Your father is below,' she told me as one of the grooms came to murmur in her ear.

In the end I had sent garments for my father and brothers that they too might appear to advantage at the reception. He was standing in the great hall, trying to look at his ease in his amber robe with its silver beading. When he saw Lady Petronella coming down the stairs with me in all my finery behind her his mouth dropped open and then he bowed and began hectoring in the manner of a man out of his milieu and determined to conceal it.

'My Lady Petronella — an honour, a most signal honour indeed. Now Zabillet, girl, I hope you are aware of the honour — the most great honour of having been chosen as bride for one of the finest men in the land. She will do me credit, Madam. I promise that she will do me credit.'

'Oh, I am sure of it, Master d'Aude,' Lady Petronella said. 'Child, I will ride ahead to join my grandson at the church door. Bring your daughter in a moment or two.'

She was wearing breeches under the split skirt of her mulberry gown, a piece of sartorial impertinence at which my conventional father would have expressed disgust had it not been the demoiselle of La Neige who flaunted it. While she mounted up my father and I stood in awkward silence. We never had much to say to each other, and now we stood like strangers.

'It is a fine day at least,' he said at

last. 'You'll not get mud on your fine new gown.'

'We are to ride down to the church,' I said.

'Ride?' He stared at me. 'Ride on horseback? Well, I'm not sure if that's the correct way for me to turn up at my daughter's wedding. Above my station so to speak.'

'Grooms are to lead the horses,' I said, knowing that he had never been on a horse in his life, and feared to make a fool of himself by tumbling off.

'Ah! Ah, now that is a different matter,' he said promptly. 'Very civil of Sir Benet to provide — you have done very well, child. Your mother and I are proud. I am proud of all my children, even of Jacques for all that he ran off to Carcassonne to display his defiance of me. 'Tis pity that he is not back well and sound. Your mother fretted that he might have been struck down by the pestilence there, but they likely never even let him in — some foolish girl he wished to enquire after, I dare say. Ah, the horses are being brought.'

He broke off his nervous chatter and we mounted and were soon being led by the grooms in their festive livery down the hill into the village and then up the track to the church where Father Hubert, having donned his cassock and stole, waited to marry me to Sir Benet La Neige. The entire population of Fromage had turned out to watch. I saw Denise, Reynaud's wife, with her first pregnancy pushing out the stomacher of her new dress, and my mother wiping away a tear, and little Marie giggling with excitement as she hopped from one foot to the next. Benet stood very straight and haughty, so obviously nobly born that I wondered for a moment what on earth I was doing there. And then the Service of Matrimony began and, like most brides be they sad or happy, I was caught up in the vows and the magic of the moment.

The wedding ring was on my finger

and the blessing had been pronounced. I was Zabillet La Neige, and for one brief and terrible instant I recalled Alain's words about the sliver of ice he had sensed within me.

We moved into the church for the Nuptial Mass while Israel, whom I had glimpsed on the edge of the crowd, sat outside to wait.

Usually after a wedding guests flocked to the domus of the bride's family, to drink wine and eat honey cake, but Lady Petronella had arranged a repast at the castle to which only a few of the villagers had been invited. For the others she had sent down wine and meat, a sheep now turning lazily on the big spit between village and valley.

As I was lifted to the saddle of the horse again I glanced at the demoiselle and surprised a look of flashing triumph on her fine-boned face.

Then we were returning to the fortress with the others following behind. My mother and little sister and Reynaud with his wife and Guillemotte and

Simon and Father Hubert and Israel. I was glad the last was invited for he had been part of my life ever since I could recall. The table on the dais had been set with dishes of meat and fish and great slabs of our local cheese and bowls of fruit and a red jelly fashioned in the shape of a castle with two sugar figures standing at each side — me and Benet, I supposed. The other serving maids — those who had not already left for their homes to be married themselves — embraced me, but I sensed a drawing away in them. Just as when I came to La Neige I had put distance between myself and the village, so now in wedding the master I was no longer of their company.

Lady Petronella was at her most gracious. She settled our guests at the table, urged them to the food, complimented my mother on her youthful looks, and generally put people at their ease. She was, in so many ways, a great lady. The atmosphere thawed as the wine circled, and Benet rose to make his speech.

'Good people,' he said, and paused to smile at me, 'it gives me joy to have you here today. The truth is that I have long loved Zabillet and am the happiest man in the world that she has agreed to be my wife. For my part I mean to be good husband to her, and so I ask you to drink to Lady Zabillet.'

That was me, I thought. I was Lady Zabillet La Neige. I sat in my wedding dress, a handsome husband at my side, my relatives pleased about my elevation, and I felt nothing at all. I was an empty doll, smiling and eating, eating and smiling.

'We shall go down into the village afterwards,' Lady Petronella said, 'to watch the dancing and merrymaking. We celebrate not only my grandson's nuptials but also our own continued freedom from the pestilence.'

'For which I believe we must thank Israel's advice,' Father Hubert said promptly. Israel raised his goblet in acknowledgement.

The meal over we went down into the village again. Despite the splendour of the reception I suspect that Guillemotte and Simon, not to mention my own family, were relieved to be out of those confines of grandeur and back in the cobbled street of Fromage where it was not necessary to speak softly or wipe one's lips after every mouthful.

They had built a great bonfire in the meadow and were dancing, making their own music as they leapt and twirled. When we arrived a cheer went up and Benet held out his hand and led me into the measure. Feet tapping, skirts and veils flying, others joined while the bonfire blazed higher and the sun sank.

I would have gone on dancing all night because when the feet are tapping the mind is stilled, but Benet had not forgotten it was our wedding night and, between two beats of the music, he swung me aside up to the saddle of his horse and led me away. At this point in the celebrations it was customary for the guests to play the fool, stealing away the bride and making the groom pay a forfeit before he could claim her again, banging together pots and pans and shouting bawdy songs, but they went on dancing and let Benet lead me off. I suppose, since I had married out of my station, they were a little ill at ease.

I was sorry because I was ill at ease myself. The excitement of the day had worn off and my grief for Alain was knocking at the doors of my heart.

When we reached the castle Benet lifted me down and walked with me across the drawbridge. The older and more sedate servants had stayed behind to clear the feast and light the lanterns, and there were bows as we came in, though I guessed they were for the young master and not for the girl he had married.

We went up the winding stairs to the little chamber where I had sobbed myself to sleep after hearing of Alain's death and I knew from the expression in the cold grey eyes that this night Benet would not be content merely to hold my hand. To be fair, why should he? He had married me and he had the right to invade me, to claim as his own what I had always denied Alain.

You are blushing, Sister, but there is a gleam of excitement in your eyes too. Have you ever wondered what it is like to lie with a man? Have you ever wished to experience that which you have renounced?

I cannot speak for women who lie down in love nor for those married to old men or men they hate. I can speak only of Benet whom I did not love but who was young enough and comely enough. There was a little pain, even a little pleasure, for the body has desires of its own that make no account of the heart. In the end it was neither good nor bad, merely something to experience. Nothing more than that.

I slept for a while, finding the close proximity of my husband not an unpleasant thing, and woke to the sounds of voices in the courtyard below. For a moment I fancied that they had garnered courage to play the fool after all, but the voices were not yelling bawdy verses. They were calling in alarm and despair.

'Something must have happened,' Benet said, snatching his clothes and pulling them on. He went out of the room and down the stairs, and I rose myself and put on my gown again, and pushed my feet into the soft slippers that I had become accustomed to wearing since I had lived at La Neige. As I descended the steps the noise grew louder, resolving itself into a cacophony of yells, screams and shouts. Had I not been able to distinguish voices that were familiar I would have sworn we had been invaded.

In the courtyard, milling about in the light from the flaring torches, villagers were calling out and weeping. My heart froze for a moment because I feared that despite all our precautions the great death had blackened someone in the midst of the festivities, but then Benet raised his hand, demanding in his hard, carrying tones,

'What the devil's afoot?'

Someone pushed his way to the front of the crowd. Father Hubert's face was streaked with dirt and blood and he shook like an ancient tree in a strong wind.

'They have burned Israel and arrested your grandmother,' he said.

'They? Who?' Benet leapt to him, gripping his arm convulsively.

'Men from the Inquisition,' Father Hubert said, 'from Carcassonne.'

I stood for only a moment, the words beating in my brain, and then with a stifled cry I picked up my skirts and fled across the drawbridge and down the steep path, past the huddled houses, to the meadows where my grandam's domus stood, where we had roasted meat and danced to celebrate my wedding.

There was meat of a different kind burning now. I smelled the sickly-sweet scent before I saw the blackened figure, still writing in the flames, and the soldiers ringing round the bonfire so none could get near. There was a man on horseback watching, and I ran to him, my hand reaching to grasp the bridle.

I heard my own voice cry in despair, 'Why? For what reason?'

The fanatical gaze of Brother Gregory dropped to my face.

'Information was laid against the Jew,' he said. 'Tales of conjuring so that the wrath of God would be diverted from this village. He denied nothing.'

'There was no trial?' My voice was a whisper. I coughed as the smoke swirled towards me.

'No trial was needful,' he told me sternly. 'Death stalks every village in France save here in Fromage. There was clear witchcraft in it.'

'There was never witchcraft,' I choked. 'He taught us cleanliness so that the plague would not strike. In other places Jews have been burnt for poisoning the wells and bringing disease. Now you will kill those who heal and prevent?'

'Did they consider that Our Blessed Lord had wrought miracles when they nailed Him to the Cross?' Brother Gregory demanded. 'Jewry and heresy are endemic in this area, and I will root them out without fear or favour whenever they are brought to my notice. I give thanks to God that one among you was not seduced into silence but came and spoke out to me boldly.'

'But who — ?' My words died away, because I knew the answer. I saw who sat a handsome horse at a little distance with a sword at his side and black treachery in his heart. I walked up to him and stood, willing him to meet my eyes.

'You have been very busy in Carcassonne, Jacques,' I said at last. 'Are the horse and the weapon the reward for your lies, your tale-bearing? Is this how you set out on your road to knighthood?'

'Someone had to do it,' he muttered, meeting my gaze reluctantly. 'It was my only chance to get away, sister.'

'Don't call me so!' I clenched my fists and beat them against his booted leg. 'I am not any sister of yours. I disown you as our parents will do. I hope that you die but not soon. First I hope that you suffer. I hope that Israel rides behind you wherever you travel in the world, and I hope that you pray for death a thousand times before it comes to you.'

'Amen to that,' said my mother's voice, as she came to my side, holding me tightly against her. Her face was swollen with weeping and there was a kind of dreary horror in her eyes. 'Master Israel saved me and Marie at her birthing, and has ever done good deeds among us. You are no son of mine. I have a son called Reynaud and no other. No other son.'

She began to weep again, still holding me, and the one who had been my brother turned and rode to join the other soldiers who ringed the hasty stake where Master Israel hung motionless at last.

At dawn the church bell tolled, calling us to worship. I had gone back to La Neige, but Benet had ridden off to discover what had happened to Lady Petronella, and those who were left huddled in the great hall, whispering, hazarding guesses as to what would happen now. Everybody, even the servants from Lorraine, obeyed the summons of the bell. Father Hubert had never had so large a congregation. But he sat at the side near the Lady Altar and it was Brother Gregory who offered the Mass.

We stood, sat, knelt in silence, and when he turned with the Host in his hands not one rose and went to the rail to partake of the Body and Blood of Our Lord. I saw Brother Gregory's face darken with anger, a vein swelling at his temple, and then he controlled himself with an effort and continued with the Sacrifice.

There was no sermon. He would ride back to Carcassonne to make his report, and it would be for others to decide what penance, if any, would be imposed upon Fromage. Perhaps he already knew that he had exceeded his authority, ignoring the Pope's orders that Jews must be protected. Perhaps one burning had slaked his lust for the time. Whatever the reason he mounted up and rode away in silence when the Mass was done, the soldiers following him, and among the soldiers the man who had been my brother.

We stood in silence, watching them go, and then we went back into the church, and Guillemotte spoke for us all when she said,

'Father, will you give us Holy Communion now? From your hands we'll take it.'

So we took the Holy Wafers and then the men went down to the meadows and took the charred bones and wrapped them in a cloth and carried them to the chair where Father

Hubert sat, and he laid his hands upon them, saying,

'My dear old friend wanted always to go to Jerusalem. I have vowed to go in his stead.'

They laid the bones beneath the Lady Altar and there they are to this day. In life he would not enter the church but in death his memory graces it.

Benet came home a week later and he brought Lady Petronella with him. She was in a fighting mood, furious at having been arrested, vowing vengeance against the fanatic Brother Gregory.

'If I have to see His Holiness myself I'll have that black crow defrocked,' she declared.

'He believed that he was doing God's work,' Father Hubert said tiredly.

'The Devil's more like,' Lady Petronella said wrathfully. ' 'Tis a sad blot in our history that we stood by, wringing our hands, and let it happen. We should have protected Master Israel as he protected us.'

'We could not stand against the soldiers,' Father Hubert said wearily. 'God knows we ought to have done, but heroism is a rare virtue. They did not hurt you, my lady?'

'They dared not,' she said with an angry little laugh. 'I wiped the floor with those who tried to question me. I reminded them that the Lords of La Neige are not accustomed to being accused of lying, of shielding Christ-killers, or of working magic. I reminded them that long since I was questioned about my beliefs and found innocent then, and it is unlawful to keep swooping on a poor woman. They let me go.'

'But too late for Israel,' Father Hubert said. 'God knows, it hurts my heart to think that he died unconverted. A stubborn man. A very stubborn man.'

'It was your brother laid the information,' Lady Petronella said, looking at me.

'He is not my brother,' I said stonily.

But it was not true. Jacques was my brother still, the lad who had always wanted to go for a soldier, who had taken the only way he knew. And in the back of my mind was the knowledge that if I had given him the bag of coins hidden in the wall of my grandam's domus Israel might be resisting conversion still. I had my own silent guilt to bear.

'I will set out for Jerusalem in the spring,' Father Hubert said. 'You know when a Jew dies it is custom to say Kadesh for him. In the Holy Land I will find a Jew to undertake that office.'

'If you ever get there,' Lady Petronella said.

'I will get there and return,' Father Hubert said. 'All that troubles me is that Fromage will be left without an incumbent priest while I am away.'

'No harm ever came from the absence of priests,' Lady Petronella said ironically. 'No doubt the Bishop will provide us with some puling minister.'

She grinned to show that she was jesting and clapped Father Hubert on the shoulder. He gave her a weary smile. I wondered how they could smile at all after what had happened and then I reminded myself that I too smiled and ate and drank and lay with Benet when my own dear love rotted in a grave somewhere in Cahors.

But Fromage had altered. The death of Master Israel had stained the landscape of our lives. We blamed ourselves and we blamed each other for having allowed it to happen, for not having stopped Jacques from going to Carcassonne. And there were others who muttered that perhaps it had been no bad thing after all, that when all was said and done Israel had sprung from an accursed race, doomed to wander. Had his death been unlawful then surely the fanatic priest would have been struck down by lightning. So the whispers grew and gathered, and within the month the first plague death had occurred among us.

My little sister Marie whose birthing had been eased by the Jew complained of a headache at noon and by sunset was dead, with the black blood suffusing her sweet face. It was like a judgement upon us. I could not weep for her, nor even go down to comfort my mother. Benet was adamant about that.

'There is infection in your mother's domus now. I forbid you to go near.'

I could have defied him and gone into the village, but the truth is that I feared death as much as anyone, and his prohibition served me as excuse for my own cowardice. But I wept for my little sister, and sent coins to Father Hubert so that he could offer Masses for her soul.

Then one morning as I sat in the solar, listlessly picking over a jumble of silks, Benet strode in, and said to me,

'You had best have someone pack your gowns, Zabillet. We are going to Paris.'

I stared at him with my mouth open,

and he went on, impatiently, 'The King has died and we have a new monarch. Philip the Sixth has given place to Jean the Second, and we are bidden to attend the Coronation. It is a great honour for our House.'

'But how will we go?' I said foolishly. 'The plague — '

'Is abating. In any case a Coronation cannot be stopped for a plague. We shall ride out tomorrow.'

'So soon?'

There would be no time to say farewell to everybody. I suppose he guessed what was in my head because he said warningly, 'I'll not have you sneaking into the village to embrace your relatives. We'll not carry the pestilence in our saddle-bags. Tell the maids to prepare your garments. We shall ride north with all speed to pay our respects.'

The Lords of La Neige had only ever been on the fringes of the Court and Benet was ambitious. I could hardly blame him for that. I was ambitious myself, and something in me mocked, 'Once the summit of your desire was to keep a tavern and now you're riding off to Court as if you were a genuine lady'.

We left the next morning, myself mounted on a palfrey with a velvet travelling-cloak over my green gown. Now that I was titled I could wear green legally. As we came across the drawbridge on to the rough ground with all the grooms crowding behind, I saw a figure standing motionless by the spring. It was my mother, come to take one last glimpse of me. She had wound a shawl about her head, and she stood very still, her eyes turned in my direction. She dared not come nearer because of the plague, but her whole heart was in her eyes as she looked at me.

I think she knew then that we would never meet again. She was losing a third child, having buried one and disowned one, and now I was riding away from her, from everybody I had known. I wanted to dismount and hug her as if I were a girl again, but fear of the pestilence held me back.

We rode away over the rough ground towards the northern road. I looked back at the crest of the hill and saw her standing there still, very small and gallant, by the spring.

11

We travelled through a dead land, with whole villages already sinking back into weed and woodland, with the tolling of the bells sounding on the air, with those other travellers whom we met turning aside, nervously covering their mouths and noses for fear of the pestilence. As we rode north the land became flatter and wetter, and the French we heard spoken in the hostelries where we slept was quite different from our own southern dialect.

And after three weeks we entered Paris. It was the first city apart from Avignon that I had seen, and for the first weeks there I moved about in a kind of daze, my ears assaulted by the noise, my nostrils offended by the stinks, my eyes constantly pulled this way, that way, by a multitude of sights.

It was said that a third of the population had died of the great plague, but there were still seventy-five thousand citizens, give or take a few, streaming through the narrow, ordure-filled streets, crying their wares at every corner, jostling, quarrelling, laughing, huddling in the corners, spitting, hawking, gaping at the heads of executed criminals that decorated the walls — I turned my own gaze away from those last sights, feeling vomit rise in my throat.

We lodged at an hotel which was considered a handsome house, but its upper storey overhung the street and the fires smoked when the wind was in the east.

I, who had longed to live in a city, was constantly wishing that I could run barefoot over green grass, and exchange greetings with people I knew. Instead I must remain within doors save when Benet or two of the grooms could escort me on some shopping expedition. Benet was a generous husband, forever buying me new kirtles and ribbons and gee-gaws. When I was dressed up with my hair elaborately braided and my eyelids painted with silver, he was proud of me. Did we go to Court? Oh, yes, Sister, we made our bows to the new king. As I had never seen a king I had nothing with which to compare him, but he was certainly as I imagined a monarch ought to look in the splendour of his robes and the smiles he bestowed on all around. There were to be receptions and hunting-parties and trips down the river but I was not able to be present. Within a month of our arrival in Paris I fell sick with nausea that lasted until noon and with fits of weeping that were quite foreign to my nature. At first Benet feared that it was some new manifestation of the pestilence, but the doctor he summoned laughed and assured us both that the sickness had a natural cause.

Some women bear their children with ease. I was unfortunate with that first pregnancy, for the constant nausea persisted and my wrists and ankles swelled and ached. It was impossible for me to go anywhere, and I spent long, tedious days cooped up in our smoky rooms, retching over the dainties the cook prepared to tempt my appetite.

'Must we stay here?' I begged Benet. 'Cannot we go into the country? You have a castle in Lorraine. Cannot we go there?'

'Upon my soul,' Benet said, fixing me with his cold, grey gaze, 'you have certainly learned how to make demands! You were born in a domus at Fromage or had you forgotten that?'

'And am now Lady La Neige,' I said impertinently. 'If you want your son to be born strong and healthy then let me leave the stink of the city and go to your castle in Lorraine.'

I was behaving very badly, I knew, but I made my condition the excuse for it. So did Benet, for after he had frowned and kept silent for an evening he told me, as if it were his own idea, that he had resolved to send me into

Lorraine where the air was fresh and I might wait out my pregnancy.

He did not offer to come with me and part of my pleasure in the journey rose from that. Oh, I cannot blame him for I married without love, but I had hoped that as my grief for Alain's death waned I might feel something stronger and sweeter for my husband than gratitude. But the truth is that there was nothing between us but courtesy. He had a toe in the Court now and spent most of his time there, and he had little patience with a pregnant, discontented wife. He bought gifts for me because he couldn't be bothered to spend his leisure with me, and I preferred the gifts to his company.

So I was escorted into Lorraine, swaying in a litter like a fine lady, with grooms and maids riding with me, and my husband, having wished me well, kissed me and turned back into the city with an unmistakable air of relief.

The nausea receded and my spirits

rose as we travelled eastward. In truth I was looking forward eagerly to being mistress in my own home, for at La Neige Lady Petronella held sway. There were still deserted villages and unploughed fields and the tolling of bells, but the great pestilence had reached its zenith, and the numbers of deaths grew fewer week by week. Which meant that the wars with England started again. Don't you find that strange, Sister, that men who had rushed to confess their sins and vowed their lives to God if they were only spared forgot every promise when the plague had passed them by and began at once to make war upon their fellow men again?

At least I would be in a comparatively peaceful place where I could bring up my child. Despite my sickness and the lack of warmth between Benet and me I loved my child long before it was born, and looked forward eagerly to rearing it.

The castle was a great stone building

set in low-lying fields, with a moat about it, and a tower at each of its four corners. It was bigger than the fortress of La Neige, but it lacked the awesome quality of that dwelling. There were bedchambers in the four towers and a long, low central hall with the kitchens at the back and a staff of servants who ran the household far more efficiently than I could ever do. I am sure they knew after one glance at me that I was of low degree, but they were well trained and polite, and never showed me anything less than respect.

My daughter was born six months after I came in to Lorraine. My pregnancy had been sheer misery but the labour itself was easy. Marget slipped into the world as easily as if she was eager to begin living as quickly as possible. Before the nine days' confinement was up I was on my feet and eating heartily.

Benet rode from Paris to see the babe, frowning doubtfully into the cradle.

'She looks screwed up,' he said at last.

'Indeed she does not,' I said indignantly. 'She has her thinking expression on.'

'Is that what it is?' He poked her gently with his finger. 'Her hair is going to be as red as yours.'

'It is not her fault,' I said.

'In Italy red hair is becoming fashionable,' Benet told me. 'It is more pity she is not a boy. My grandmother wanted a great-grandson, you know.'

'I did not have a girl merely to disoblige her,' I said coldly.

'Of course you did not.' Benet laughed and put his arm about my waist. 'I will stay home for a while, I think.'

'What you mean,' I said crisply, 'is that you will stay until you get me with child again.'

'Something like that,' he said and kissed me carelessly.

The castle was different when the

master was home. The servants moved more swiftly; the food came to the table hot; after supper there were visitors who came to renew their old acquaintance with my husband. It was then that I realised Benet was not quite as rich as I had supposed. Oh, compared with the peasants from whom I sprang he was very rich indeed, but much of his wealth came from the dice and gambling in which he indulged with his cronies. And he did not always win. Many was the night when one or other of his companions rode home with their saddle-bags weighed down with silver plate and gold coin.

'Your grandam would not be pleased to know how casually you squander your wealth,' I said one night after his visitors had won more than usual from him in their games of chance.

'My grandmother is an old crow,' he said rudely, 'who grudges me innocent pleasure. And who will run with tales to her? Will you?'

I shook my head.

'Then have the goodness to mind your own affairs,' he told me. 'I'm a grown man and spend my money as I choose. You cannot complain that you are kept short.'

That was true enough. He had brought me a gown of silver cloth from Paris as a reward for Marget.

'Give me a boy next year and the cloth will be of gold,' he promised.

'You may have to keep your promise,' I said gloomily, 'for I was sick this morning.'

'And Marget scarcely six weeks old!' The irritation in his face widened into a delighted smile.

'I am fertile it seems,' I said, but there was pride as well as resignation in my voice. As I did not love my husband I hoped instead to fill the emptiness of my heart with children. And for all the gifts he gave me I doubted if Benet was deeply in love with me either, for as soon as my second pregnancy had been confirmed he rode away again to Paris. When he had gone the servants relaxed again, doing their tasks more slowly, but I let them be. I was only a sparrow dressed up as a peacock and they knew it as well as I did.

And did I, in all this time, ever think of Alain? Every day, usually when I was occupied with some task that busied my hands and failed to engage my thought, then he was in my mind. His dark eyes under the thatch of silver-fair hair, his tanned skin and broad shoulders, the tiny cleft in his chin, were as clear in my memory as when we had sat by my grandmother's domus and planned our marriage. And sometimes I woke in the morning with a feeling of remembered joy because in my sleep I had dreamed of him, living still and loving me.

A few days after my twentieth birthday I bore my second child. It was a boy, and he came roaring into the world with his eyes screwed tightly shut and his miniature fists clenched. When he opened his eyes they were grey like his father's and his hair was as dark. I named him Jean after my own father, and wondered how long it would be before Benet grew weary of Court gaieties and went south again. The truth was that I was homesick, I suppose. The gentle landscape of Lorraine, the handsome castle, the two babes didn't fill my days. I had no friends. Word that Benet La Neige had married beneath him had been broadcast and when he returned to the city my evenings were without visitors.

Benet brought me the gown of golden cloth and only frowned a little when he learned that I had called the baby after my father instead of his own. What pleased him was that the boy looked like him just as Marget was myself in miniature.

'Can we go to La Neige soon?' I asked, hopefully.

'In a year or two, when the children are of an age to travel,' he evaded, and I heaved a silent sigh, guessing that the excitements of Court life held him fast.

He went back to Paris soon afterwards, thankfully without leaving me pregnant, and I settled down with what patience I could to rear my children and try to mature into the role of lady of the manor into which I had entered upon my marriage.

Season blended into season, and now and then Benet came to spend a month or two. Any hope I had entertained of love-liking growing between us quickly faded. Once he had his son he never troubled to touch me, and from one or two remarks he let drop I suspected that he was keeping company with Anne Foix again for all that she was now married to someone else. I was not even jealous which will prove to you that I really didn't love him. But I was grateful for the comforts with which he provided us. The babes were cosseted and cherished, and little by little I grew accustomed to the cushioned solitude of my existence. Marget was six and Jean five when Benet came unexpectedly to tell me that a message had come from Fromage to inform him that the Lady Petronella was failing, and wished to see her great-grandchildren before she died.

'It is right that we should go,' I said eagerly. 'We ought to have gone before this time.'

'You don't enjoy being mistress here?' he asked sardonically.

'The master is too often away,' I muttered, but the truth was that I doubt if he would have been made welcome had he come too often. There were times when I could pretend that he had ceased to exist or gone abroad for more years than I could count.

We set out almost at once. It saddened me as we rode to see the crops still despoiled and villages run back into wasteland. Even after five years France was still torn and bleeding. As we neared the south I felt my spirits rise as if I were a girl again. The very air smelled sweeter and it seemed to me that even the wind blew more gently.

But there was sadness too. My

mother had died of the pestilence soon after we had first entered Paris. A messenger had brought the news three months afterwards, but I had not wept. I had known when she stood by the spring to watch me ride out that we wouldn't meet again.

'You are not unhappy with me, are you?' Benet asked suddenly.

He had edged his mount close to mine out of hearing of the grooms and the children. His question startled me so much that I gaped at him. It was rare for him to make a remark that smacked of intimacy.

'No,' I said at last, and it was true. I was not happy, but happiness had died for me in the pestilence, and Benet was a good husband, according to his lights.

'I would have you tell my grandmother that, if she asks,' he said.

'Yes, of course,' I said, at a loss to understand why he suddenly wished to present us as a devoted couple.

And then the matter passed from my

mind for as we reached the next hill I recognised the landscape and cried out with pleasure to see the high tower of La Neige pointing into the sky. Had I been alone I would have ridden down into the village to see everybody at once, but those days were long gone, and now I must ride sedately over the drawbridge and dismount with grace, the servants coming to greet us.

'Is Lady Petronella still alive?' I asked, and was assured by half a dozen voices that she was brighter this day than she had been for a long time. She was seated in a high-backed chair near the blazing fire for though it was summer logs were burning in the huge central hearth. Her face was thickly painted; her hands flashed jewels; only her eyes were alive in the white bones of her face.

'So you gave me great-grandchildren,' she said, and Marget and Jean ventured closer and stood at each side of her, two rosebuds against a withered tree.

'They are pretty children,' she allowed.

'Now that I have seen them I can die in peace.'

'You are not going to die for a long time, my lady,' I said rallyingly, but she cut me short, her voice impatient.

'Don't treat me like an idiot, Zabillet. It is high time that I died. I am past sixty and too vain to tell you how far past. I have a pain that eats in my side and whispers to me of death. Tomorrow I will embark upon the endura as a good Cathar should.'

'There are no Cathars now,' I told her. 'That heresy is dead.'

'Not until I am gone, child.' She bared her yellow teeth in a skeleton grin. 'Do you want me to linger for many weeks in pain? No, after today no food or water shall pass my lips, and you will oblige me by not sending for a priest. I'll have no Roman mumbo-jumbo to chant me into heaven.'

'If Father Hubert were here — ' I began.

'Father Hubert vanished in the Holy Land,' she broke in. 'The old fool was likely murdered by the Saracens. Your mother died — did they tell you?'

I nodded, biting my lip.

'Your father drinks,' she said flatly. 'He loved your mother well, and after she died he was without pride or hope. Your brother Reynaud works the land now. His Denise gave him five children and there's another on the way. Of Jacques there was never word.'

'I know nobody of that name,' I said stonily. 'As for the endura, why we'll not have it.'

'You are grown a fine lady, aren't you, with your will and will nots?' she mocked. 'I am still Demoiselle of La Neige and manage my own affairs in dying or living. Now bring stools for the little ones for their company gives me joy. They are the future for which I planned.'

I had tried to warn both Marget and Jean that the Lady Petronella was very old and somewhat sharp in manner, but I need not have fretted. The very old and the very young hold eternity in common and they chatted to her as if they had always known her. As we broke bread and drank wine I listened and thought it possible that in her pleasure in their company she might forget her resolve and fight to live.

I was rising from the table with the intention of slipping down into the village when her voice checked me.

'Attend me to my bed, Zabillet. I wish to speak to you.'

She was too weak to walk but as the servants lifted her in the great chair and carried her up the winding steps she held her head as proudly as a queen. Benet had risen to attend her too, but she waved an imperious hand, saying,

'It is Zabillet I wish to see. Show your younglings over La Neige.'

In the bedchamber space where the huge, high bed waited to receive her I stood while she was transferred from the chair. Though the servants lifted her gently I felt rather than heard her wince and pity struggled with my affection.

'Go away, all of you. Child, come and sit near to me. I have a tale to tell,' she ordered.

I went close, seating myself on a stool by the cushions among which she was enthroned.

'Are you happy with my grandson?' she asked.

'He is a good husband,' I said cautiously.

'Don't prevaricate!' she said curtly. 'He treats you well?'

'He is most generous,' I said truthfully.

'He is a weak fool under his posturing,' she said. 'His father was weak too. My son had no backbone, no interest in La Neige or in the family. He married against my wishes — a girl as feeble as himself. When they both died there was relief mingled with my grief. Now I had the rearing of my grandson. I had high hopes for the boy but they were not justified. He had the arrogance and the air but not the true nobility. He has always been a handsome shell.'

'He is a good husband,' I repeated, feeling an obscure need to stand up for him.

'I said that I was going to tell you a tale — a true tale,' Lady Petronella said. 'A tale of a young girl with red hair and a proud tilt to her chin. A peasant, but intelligent, healthy — worth a dozen weak and inbred girls. Too much inbreeding weakens the stock, you know.' It was her pet theory. I wondered why she was trotting it out all over again.

'I made up my mind that we needed fresh blood in the line,' Lady Petronella said. 'When I told you there was a place for you here that was by way of test, girl. I fancied I saw the cold spark of ambition in you, and I was right, wasn't I? Not for you the early marriage, the babes born too soon. You wanted to better yourself. That was why you kept putting off the shepherd lad and in the end you didn't marry him after all.'

'Alain died,' I reminded her.

'The lad didn't die,' Lady Petronella said.

I jerked upright, staring at her. The words were jumping about on the surface of my mind, not penetrating my understanding. I said, dry-mouthed,

'There was a letter came.'

'Which you couldn't read. It was to tell you he was well, that the pestilence had passed him by. He'd had a clerk write it. He said he was staying in Cahors and not bringing the flock here that spring, but that he'd be here the next spring with a ring for your wedding.'

She had read words that were not written, had burned the missive at my request, had used what came to hand to serve her own ends.

I said, gently, carefully,

'Does Benet know?'

'Of course not. He knows nothing,' she said impatiently.

'Did — Alain return?'

'The following spring. By that time you were safely wed and in Paris.'

'How did — ?'

'He came here, demanding explanation. Oh, there was spirit in the lad. He wanted to know how such a tale could have arisen.'

'And you told him — ?' How small and cool my voice was.

'I told him that you had fallen in love with my grandson, that you had spun a story of Alain's dying that your family might not think you unfaithful. Your mother might have given him the lie but she was dead by then and the Jew burned and Father Hubert gone into the Holy Land. There were none to vouch for your truthfulness. There were none to say that if you had said he was dead it could only have been because you believed it yourself.'

'What did he do?'

'He went away again with his sheep. By now he may be dead in truth.'

She sounded so calm, I thought, as if she were relating a tale that had nothing whatsoever to do with either of us. She had taken my life and broken

304

it in her hands and she seemed not to know or care.

'Why did Benet marry me?' I asked abruptly. 'He had no real desire to wed at all, let alone a peasant maid in whom his grandmother took an interest.'

'I hinted to him that I was leaving La Neige to you. Naturally he married you so that he would inherit. Benet may be weak but he's not entirely a fool.'

'And have you?' I asked harshly.

'My dear Zabillet, of course not.' She gave the little, creaking laugh of old age. 'Do you seriously imagine that I would will La Neige to a peasant?'

I saw it all then, clear, sharp, ugly. She had planned ahead, twisting events to bring about the end she craved.

'Why tell me now?' I said dully.

'They would have told you when you went down into the village that Alain was alive. I thought it only fair that you should understand the reasons for my actions.'

'I'm no priest,' I said, rising. 'You

have no need to make confession to me, but it isn't a confession, is it? You are not sorry for what you did. You are not sorry at all.'

'Sorry?' She frowned slightly. 'No, should I be? You are Lady La Neige now. You have two homes, a fine son and daughter, lovely clothes, and a husband who is generous. Would you have done better for yourself, wed to the shepherd lad?'

'If you wish to enter into the endura,' I said, 'then I'll not seek to persuade you otherwise.' Better she should die of thirst and starvation as quickly as possible. Better she had never laid eyes on a red-headed girl running through the meadow. Perhaps in some part of herself she wanted forgiveness. If so then I had none to give. I gave her one long hard look, and turned and went down the stairs again.

Benet was just coming through the main door with Marget and Jean holding his hands and chattering to him. He was a good father, I thought, looking down at them. He was not a bad husband, and he had been cheated too, driven to marry me to secure his inheritance. He would not be pleased when he found out there had been no need to marry me at all.

Of Alain I could not begin to think with any composure. I had accepted with pain the fact of his death, but I could not suddenly make him alive again in my head.

The next morning Lady Petronella embarked upon the endura, a stubborn Cathar to the end. The young priest who had taken over from Father Hubert came up to the castle to offer the Last Rites and was embarrassed and upset when his services were rejected. She died three days later, and in that time I never went near. There was nothing in me but a cold, hard anger.

When the Will was read it was Benet's turn for anger. I sat, clasping my hands tightly together, waiting for the explosion. Now he would know that his grandmother had tricked him into wedlock with a peasant by pretending she was willing La Neige away from the family. No explosion came. I had underestimated his habit of self-control. He drew breath in a hiss but made no other move, though his grey eyes chilled to ice.

'She was always set on getting her own way,' he said at last.

'I knew nothing of it,' I told him. 'She said nothing until the very end.'

'I need not have married you at all.'

He rose and went over to one of the windows, gazing out into the courtyard.

'Alain Berger is not dead,' I said.

'The shepherd lad?' He turned sharply, looking at me.

The children were abed and we had dismissed the servants.

'She lied about that too,' I said.

To my surprise he came over and put his hand on my shoulder.

'I'm sorry, Zabillet,' he said. 'I didn't know. I didn't guess.'

'What are we going to do?' I asked.

'I am not unhappy in our marriage,' he said slowly. 'You have given me two fine children.'

'But there is no loving between us,' I said.

'How much love is there between most married couples?' he asked lightly.

'I suppose not.' I unclasped my hands and sent him a pleading glance. 'Benet, I don't want to go on living with you. It is not your fault. Nor mine either.'

There was a long silence then. It was as if with the revelation of all the lies whatever of affection had been between us had died and been buried like Lady Petronella.

'You don't want me,' I said. 'You never really did. These past years you devote the hours you are not gambling to Anne Foix. You don't want me, Benet.'

'A marriage cannot be dissolved,' he said tightly.

'But you need not feel obliged to live with me. You have a position at Court, friends in the north — '

'You wish to stay here at La Neige? To take my grandmother's place?'

'To stay here anyway. It was always my home,' I said. 'You can ride down to visit your estate. There need be no open breach.'

'It is time for Jean to be breeched and to begin his squire's training.'

'Bring him with you when you visit,' I said. 'Leave Marget with me.'

So it was settled between us without any hard words. To do Benet justice he accepted the fact that I had been cheated as he had been, and that no good would come of a quarrel. After another week he turned for the north again, taking Jean with him. That hurt my heart, to see my little boy riding off with his father. I had no fear that Benet would treat him unkindly; he was more likely to spoil him with over-indulgence, but when they came south again he would wear tunic and hose and carry a little dagger, and the baby I had loved would be gone for ever.

The day after their going I walked down into the village for the first time. We had held a service for Lady Petronella in the disused chapel within the castle and buried her beneath the flagstones there, so nobody from the village had come. Why should they indeed? She had always held herself aloof from the common people, save on the rare occasions when she needed to use one of them for her own purposes.

In the cobbled street nothing had changed; everything had changed. The neighbours came out to greet me — Jules, Guillemotte, the girls grown into stout matrons now, the lads settled into men. There was no change save the passing of the years in them. The change was in me. I had moved away from my own kind and never settled into the life of a lady.

My father came to the door of the domus and stared at me dully. He had been drinking. I saw it in his bloodshot eyes and the slight trembling of his hand.

'You've grown a fine woman, Zabillet,' he said, slurring my name.

'You've two grandchildren now, Father,' I said in a rallying tone. 'Jean and Marget.'

'And your brother Reynaud has sired a brood,' he said. 'We hear nothing of Jacques. If I'd let him go for a soldier maybe he'd not have betrayed the Jew, eh?'

'I don't know, Father,' I said. 'I don't know.'

And I walked on down past the track that led to the church, to the meadows where Benet had ridden with a hawk on his wrist, and Israel had writhed in the flames, and a red-haired girl had sat with a shepherd lad planning the future.

The domus, my domus, still stood with the roof half ruined and the door hanging by one hook. I stood and looked at it, and felt the salt tears of my vanished girlhood run down my face, and then I turned and walked slowly up the long hill to the castle again.

Other titles in the Linford Romance Library

SAVAGE PARADISE
Sheila Belshaw

For four years, Diana Hamilton had dreamed of returning to Luangwa Valley in Zambia. Now she was back — and, after a close encounter with a rhino — was receiving a lecture from a tall, khaki-clad man on the dangers of going into the bush alone!

PAST BETRAYALS
Giulia Gray

As soon as Jon realized that Julia had fallen in love with him, he broke off their relationship and returned to work in the Middle East. When Jon's best friend, Danny, proposed a marriage of friendship, Julia accepted. Then Jon returned and Julia discovered her love for him remained unchanged.

PRETTY MAIDS ALL IN A ROW
Rose Meadows

The six beautiful daughters of George III of England dreamt of handsome princes coming to claim them, but the King always found some excuse to reject proposals of marriage. This is the story of what befell the Princesses as they began to seek lovers at their father's court, leaving behind rumours of secret marriages and illegitimate children.

THE GOLDEN GIRL
Paula Lindsay

Sarah had everything — wealth, social background, great beauty and magnetic charm. Her heart was ruled by love and compassion for the less fortunate in life. Yet, when one man's happiness was at stake, she failed him — and herself.

DARBY, C.   F

Zabillet of the snow

∠MH	KENILWORTH COMMUNITY SERVICES		2 5 JUL 2012
			MALIN
Mytun			2 NOV 2010
-4 SEP 2009		2 4 NOV 2011	1 4 JAN 2011
Shorthood Corbra			
Winn Lee		3 0 JAN 2012 MAR 2011	
Webb		8 -	- 4 APR 2011
Geadhead FEB 2011	- 2 SEP 2011		Lander Hz
1 4 MAY 2012		1 6 MAR 2012	0 OCT 2011

This item is to be returned or renewed on or before the latest date
above. It may be borrowed for a further period if not in demand.
To renew items call in or phone any Warwickshire library, or renew
on line at www.warwickshire.gov.uk/wild

Discover • Imagine • Learn • *with libraries*

www.warwickshire.gov.uk/libraries

Warwickshire
County Council

0129517484

SPECIAL MESSAGE TO READERS

This book is published under the auspices of

THE ULVERSCROFT FOUNDATION

(registered charity No. 264873 UK)

Established in 1972 to provide funds for research, diagnosis and treatment of eye diseases. Examples of contributions made are: —

A Children's Assessment Unit at Moorfield's Hospital, London.

•

Twin operating theatres at the Western Ophthalmic Hospital, London.

•

A Chair of Ophthalmology at the Royal Australian College of Ophthalmologists.

•

The Ulverscroft Children's Eye Unit at the Great Ormond Street Hospital For Sick Children, London.

You can help further the work of the Foundation by making a donation or leaving a legacy. Every contribution, no matter how small, is received with gratitude. Please write for details to:

**THE ULVERSCROFT FOUNDATION,
The Green, Bradgate Road, Anstey,
Leicester LE7 7FU, England.
Telephone: (0116) 236 4325**

In Australia write to:

**THE ULVERSCROFT FOUNDATION,
c/o The Royal Australian College of
Ophthalmologists,
27, Commonwealth Street, Sydney,
N.S.W. 2010.**

ZABILLET OF THE SNOW

For Zabillet, a young peasant girl growing up in the tiny French village of Fromage in the mid-fourteenth century, a respectable marriage is the height of her parents' ambitions for her. But life is changing. Zabillet's love for a handsome shepherd is tested when she is invited to join the La Neige household, where her mistress, Lady Petronella, has plans for her grandson, Benet. And over all broods the horror of the Great Death that claims all whom it touches.

Books by Catherine Darby
in the Linford Romance Library:

FROST ON THE MOON